THE
WANDERERS

NAMELESS - BOOK ONE
NIKKI ROBB

THE WANDERERS

NAMELESS - BOOK ONE

NIKKI ROBB

CONTENT WARNINGS

This novel includes and alludes to things that may be concerning such as murder, vampires, blood drinking, graphic sex, sexual assault, rape, cancer, death of a parent and family member, non-consensual sexual encounters, victim-blaming, panic attacks, PTSD, discrimination, hate crimes, parental neglect, and disowning.

Please consider these before continuing.

ACKNOWLEDGMENTS

I have to give a huge shout out to all my friends and family for being such amazing supportive pillars in my creative life. My husband, Zack, for always being my first beta reader, my mom for her continued support and Mariah for the creative energy that you always elicit in me.

If you are in my family, thank you so much for picking up this book and supporting me. Truly, it means so much to me. Now, please put this book down and don't read it. I mean it. Please. This isn't for you. This novel will not make good conversation over the Thanksgiving dinner table. I'm not above begging. Please. Thank you.

To all of you who grew up loving sexy vampires. I hope you are ready for the supernatural ride of a lifetime.

To those of you who wanted Bella to get down and
dirty with ALL of the Cullens.

ATHENA

PROLOGUE

You've read the stories and heard the tales about the things that go bump in the night, the monsters under your bed and in your closet. It's all pretty terrifying stuff to hear as you're growing up, never really feeling safe. You probably spent most of your childhood constantly checking every nook and cranny in your house, looking around every corner for what vicious and violent creature might be lurking there, poised to attack.

Growing up, and especially growing up as a woman, you learn two unsettling things pretty quickly in life.

One, the monsters from those stories aren't real.

Two, the monsters in the real world are even more terrifying.

Men don't need claws to claim a woman's unwilling flesh. Men don't need inhuman strength to pin a woman down. Men don't need fangs to drain a woman's life. Men don't have to be invisible, they don't have to hide in order to lure us to their traps.

No, sometimes, men are vile monsters all on their own.

That's the unfortunate truth though, isn't it? The lesson we were taught by

Scooby Doo every week on TV. The unsettling fact that we all had to come to terms with as we grew and saw the truth of the world for the first time.

The real monsters are human.

ATHENA

ONE

Living in the middle of Nowhere, Maine sucks. For three months of the year, our little town of Shockgrove becomes a tourist playground, with crab shacks on every corner, and live music every night. For those few months, all the ridiculously expensive beach houses that stand empty every other month of the year are packed with housewives who are joined by their husbands on the weekends, college kids with big bank accounts and reckless attitudes, and those families who are rich enough to afford three months away from their jobs, duties, and lives to spend an entire summer drinking, swimming, and sunbathing.

During those three months, business is great, the economy booms, and my family's bookstore cafe becomes a hotspot that tourists just can't get enough of. We're right there on the pier, a perfect sanctuary on rainy days, or days when the sun's warmth is just too powerful for some of the newer visitors. They'd stop inside for tea, an iced coffee, and a good book. My family has owned this little shop for three generations. My Grandma and her husband started it back in the 50s when they would sell a cup of coffee for 75 cents. Then my mother took it on after Grandpa passed and Grandma just couldn't do it alone anymore, although she still spent most of her time in the shop. Citing that 'nobody can do it the right way anymore.'

It was only Mom and me for as long as I could remember. She never told me much about my dad, as far as I'm concerned he was a sperm donor who didn't deserve another moment of my time. Mom remarried once, but I tried not to think about that anymore. My stepfather was now in prison, where he belonged. Despite the many changes that occurred throughout our lives, this coffee shop-slash-bookstore was the one constant. The Maine Plotline was a Landry family business, and for three months of the year, business was good. Great even.

For the other nine months of the year, however, it was a ghost town, with a measly population of just over five-thousand people, and business frankly suffered. Not many people call little coastal towns like this home. It's always the stop along the way, the blip in the timeline of family memories, not the destination. But to me, Shockgrove was my beginning, middle, and likely my end.

It's like a vacuum, this town, and its people. I've tried to leave, trust me. Dozens of times. During sophomore year, my world turned on its axis. Sending me into a spiral I've fought tooth and nail every day since to climb out of. Trying to get out of this town at any and every opportunity. I applied to some stupid all-girls boarding school. Not that I would have minded being without men. I wanted nothing to do with men and their depraved desires for a long time. An all-girls school seemed like a dream I would never be allowed to have. Plus, it was obvious that I was bisexual at age fourteen when I first saw The Mummy and I wasn't sure if I wanted Brendan, Rachel or to be between them. I would have been fine with all women. Great, even. However, I didn't take into account the price of a boarding school education so that was promptly shut down. That, and Mom needed me at the shop. We couldn't afford staff, so for the longest time, it was just me and her, with Grandma when she could.

Senior year, I planned on heading away for college like so many of my classmates were going to do, but life had other plans. That's when Mom got sick.

The best thing about Pancreatic cancer is that it's quick. She didn't suffer for long, and considering how much pain she was in for the short and fast end of her life, I could see that as a pro. But suddenly, The Maine Plotline was my responsibility. Grandma helped as much as she could, but she was getting older and she couldn't do as much as she wanted to. It was up to me to keep the business alive. It took me nearly two years longer than normal, but I got my business degree online while working full-time. And all of a sudden, I was twenty-six years old living in a small coastal town with a store that was practically bleeding money, and no way to escape.

I allot twenty minutes a day to feel sorry for myself about my lack of direction and passion in my life. From the moment I lock the doors at the end of the day, to the moment I finish cleaning and counting the day's drawers and leave out the back. That was it. During those few lonely minutes, I let myself lament about how I got stuck in this reality. I allow myself to dream about a life beyond this store, to dream about having more.

But the moment I walk out into the Maine evening air, the salty-sweet smell of the ocean prickling my lips, I lock away those thoughts until their cage would open again the next day.

That was how I lived my life.

I had just finished my daily mental sob fest and began the trek to my bike that was parked behind our building when my phone rang. I smiled at the name and answered, pinching the phone between my ear and my shoulder as I unlocked my bike.

"I had the literal best sex of my life last night with that guy I met at the Craving Crab. You know, the one whose address I sent you in case I went missing and you had to avenge my death. Well, I'm happy to report that the only thing I was dying of was too many orgasms. Yes, you heard me, this man had me quaking. I think I saw God. Anyway, he's going out again tonight but his friend's in town now, so he's bringing him along…" I flinched, knowing what was coming next. "So, you're going with me to keep his friend company so I can once again delve into the wondrous world of this man's cock without his stupid friend vagina-blocking." I'm pretty sure that was all in one breath. I chuckled. That was par for the course for my best friend. She's another victim of the Shockgrove vacuum. Her parents run the amusement park down on the edge of the pier and she's been doing most of the social media and event planning for them since she could hold a phone in her hand. She was good at it and even had a few TikTok videos go viral last year. Under her suggestion, they held a winter wonderland event that brought a few tourists in for the weekend. I knew the jump to social media was what The Maine Plotline was missing, but I didn't understand a single thing about marketing in that sense. Numbers and invoices, I got. Ring lights and trends, I did not. Davia offered to start a few pages for me, to even run them, but I knew I wouldn't be able to pay her what she was worth, so I never took her up on it.

"Hello to you too, Davia." I slipped the lock into my bag and straddled the seat of my bike, riding off along the dock. It was early May so the sun had only just set, basking my ride in a pink-orange hue. The tourists would be coming back in a few weeks, and not a second too soon if the store's financials were any indication.

"Yes, sorry. Hello, Athena. How are you?" She didn't wait for me to respond. "So be ready in an hour, ok?"

"I don't know, girl. I'm pretty beat." It was the truth, but more so than that, I wasn't really into the whole clubbing scene anymore. Especially not the Craving Crab, one of the only bars that stayed open through the off-season. It was always packed with locals during this time of year and you couldn't let loose with your neighbors breathing down your neck.

"You are not," she said matter of factly.

"Yes, I am," I teased back.

"I'm pulling the Vagina card." I nearly dropped the phone from between my shoulder and ear. Gripping the handles with one hand, I freed the other to rescue the falling device and pressed it firmly back to my ear.

"I'm sorry, the what?" I exclaimed.

"The Vagina card, I'm pulling it."

"And what the fuck is a Vagina card?" I said through a bout of laughter.

"You know, when you are the only thing standing in the way of my vagina and night full of mind-blowing orgasms, I can pull this so you have to help me," she spoke confidently like this was something that made perfect sense and she wasn't making it up entirely on the spot.

"You're ridiculous," I laughed, as I reached the edge of the pier and headed down the sidewalk toward my home. I smiled weakly as I rode past the lighthouse that sat tucked on the rocky shoreline. The faded white and blue tower was massive, standing out brightly against the dark black of the rocky cliff on which it made its home. It had been long since out of service after the last keeper of the lighthouse passed nearly a decade ago. It's supposed to be closed to the public, and it is, but Mom and I used to sneak up to the gallery and watch the stars at night, listening to the waves crash against the cliff below. It was our place. Right up to the very end.

Passing this lighthouse was the best and worst part of my everyday routine. On the plus side, I could feel her here. Her memory, our adventures.

On the downside, I could feel her here. Her pain, her death.

"Come on, you know I'd do the same for you!" She cried out, desperation lacing every word. That must have been some damn good dick.

I rolled my eyes, pulling them from the lighthouse and its ghosts, knowing that she wouldn't have to do anything of the sort for me anytime soon. I wasn't a virgin, unfortunately, but I certainly didn't have what you'd call an active sex life either unless you count my several vibrators at home that I used by myself.

It took me a while to feel comfortable sharing my body with anyone. And then after Mom died, I found the process of hooking up with random tourists whom I'd never see again quite pointless. Everything is temporary. Even pleasure.

"Please, Athena…Please!" I could practically picture her large brown puppy dog eyes and her thick lips pouting. She was a master of manipulation.

"Fine," I sighed as I turned the handles of my bike into my driveway. It was a long gravel road, you couldn't see my house from the main road and I liked it that way. My small cottage was nestled in a small grove of lush trees, whose newly formed leaves were a promise of a warm summer to come. The dark blue paint on the siding of my house came into view and I smiled. The one-floor cottage had two bedrooms, a kitchen, a living room, a laundry room, and one full bathroom. It wasn't much, in fact, it was the only thing I could afford after Mom passed and I sold the family home to cover expenses from having The Maine Plotline closed for two months. But it was home.

"You're amazing! Ugh, maybe we'll both get some seriously life-changing sex tonight." Not likely. Besides, I'd had 'life-changing' sex before, and I didn't want anything like that again. Ever. "I'll be there to pick you up in forty-five minutes," Davia cheered before hanging up.

I parked my bike in the small shed off the side of the cottage and made my way inside. Tossing a frozen meal into the microwave, I stopped by the baby blue record player that sat on a shelf in my living room. I threw on one of Mom's old records and felt the melancholic fog claim my heart.

The dulcet tones of Cyndi Lauper echoed through the house when I arrived home from a long day at school. Dropping my bookbag onto the bench in the foyer, a smile spread across my lips. When I came around the corner I saw my Mom dancing in front of her baby blue record player, her bare feet moving back and forth across the tile floor as she danced along to her favorite album of all time, "She's So Unusual." She sang along loudly, and badly. I did not get my slightly better-than-mediocre vocal talents from her, that's for sure. I wasn't phenomenal, but I could at least carry a tune. Her long red hair was naturally wavy, her beauty was effortless, something I appreciated, and hated about her. I had to spend a half-hour every morning trying to look as naturally radiant as she always did. She wore a loose-fitting, flowy floral shirt under jean overalls, not unlike Donna from the movie Mamma Mia, but she swore up and down that she 'wore it first'. A glass of white wine was pinched between her fingers and she swayed to the music. I leaned against the wall and watched her. For one song, then another. She noticed me somewhere between "When You Were Mine" and "Time After Time." Her off-key lyrics grew louder as she urged me to join in. I rolled my eyes, trying to shake my head, but her hand was gripping my arm and pulling me from the wall. Then we were dancing. Our voices blended in a glorious symphony of love and happiness, our bodies swaying joyfully to the music. Cares and worries slipped away when we were together.

You always hear people say that they wished they had enjoyed the people they lost a little more before they were gone. Wished that they'd loved them harder, appreciated them deeper, or made the most of the time that they had. Not me. I don't have a single regret about how I loved her. She was my everything, and I made every single second with her count. So no, I don't wish I had loved her harder, I wished I could have loved her longer.

With the music soaring through the halls, I made my way to my bedroom. A king-size bed took up the majority of the space, but I did have a very small walk-in closet where I had a vanity space. I actually loved playing around with makeup, I always had the best Halloween looks. In another life, I might have been a makeup artist. The life where I got lucky enough to get out of this town.

I spent the 10 minutes my food needed to heat up painting my features. I settled for a black and gold smokey eye with winged liner. Letting the smudged shadow frame under the eye as well. That sort of look always made me feel so confident. Like armor.

I skipped the foundation but went in with a little contour and concealer to give myself some semblance of bone structure. I ran my fingers over the small plastic case of my favorite red lipstick. I'd put it on after I ate. I didn't have much time left to do anything special with the mop of red hair on my head, so I pulled it back into a sleek ponytail and called it a day.

Forty minutes and a frozen personal pizza later, I was finished getting ready. I stood awkwardly in front of the full-length mirror on my closet door examining my outfit.

I'd pulled out something comfortable and safe. A pair of dark leggings and a Shockwave Community College crewneck sweater with the sleeves rolled up. My outfit was a large contrast to the dark and sultry makeup look I was sporting, but I liked makeup…and I normally hate dressing up. So this seemed like a good compromise. At least I put on a thong.

Not that I was expecting anything to happen tonight.

The knock on my door told me Davia had arrived, so I padded across my living room in my white Vans and opened the door.

My best friend was a knockout. Her long blonde balayage hair had been curled and effortlessly fell down her back and over her shoulders to just below her breasts. Speaking of those, she was wearing a full-blown corset. The dark red bustier barely held her C cups in. Her legs were hugged by tight leather leggings and she finished off the look with red heels. She looked like she was either about to do a strip tease, or go on stage in Vegas. Or do a strip tease in Vegas. There was a brief time in high school when I had a crush on my best friend. It was an annoying two months of not knowing how to act around her, and not knowing if she was bi. I eventually told her, and her exact words here, 'I'd be literally so offended if you weren't turned on by me, and girl you know I'd rock your world if I was into vagina.' I got over my crush and knew she'd be my best friend forever.

"You cannot wear that," she said, taking in my comfortable appearance. She brushed past me, her heels clicking against the wooden floor of my cottage.

"And why not?" I asked. "It's not like the Craving Crab is a nightclub. It's a local bar. There's pool playing, not pole dancing." I smirked, and she waved her hand as if to say I was being ridiculous.

"You need to look enticing enough to keep Greg's friend interested," she called over her shoulder on her way to my bedroom.

"I did my makeup," I retorted.

"And you look great, babe, which is why-" she mumbled from the room, "you need to be wearing this." She re-emerged from my bedroom with one of the few dresses I own. Of course. It was a dark purple body con, it barely covered my ass and the criss-cross design on the front was a far cry from modest. Davia bought it for me, and I tried it on exactly once and then buried it in the back of my closet never to be seen again. How the hell did she find it so fast?

"No way," I exclaimed, tossing my hands up as she approached.

"Yes way," she said, quickly grabbing the hem of my sweatshirt and pulling it over my head. Not exactly the best way to have my clothes ripped off of me. Although, not the worst either. I shivered, convincing myself it was from the cool air against my exposed skin and not the memory that echoed inside my head.

Once I was standing in front of my friend in nothing but my plain black bra, and she clicked her tongue.

"You don't have any better bra than that?" Her eyes scanned my body and I felt exposed in a not-fun way.

"Just give me back my sweatshirt," I cried, crossing my arms in front of me. She shook her head and pulled the purpled fabric down over my head and onto my torso. I groaned but ultimately shimmied into the dress. I pulled my leggings down, feeling the phantom wind nipping at my exposed legs.

"It's cold," I whined. Davia was already walking to my front closet and pulling out my favorite black leather jacket. I shrugged it on, and sighed, attempting to pull the skirt of the dress lower, only to show off more of my cleavage in the process. Looks like I needed to make a choice between showing off my ass or tits tonight. I saw her reach for a pair of black bootie heels and I nearly yelled after her, "No. If I'm gonna wear this outfit, I'm at least going to have comfortable shoes on." She looked down at my feet, studying the white vans.

"Fine, good enough." Then she made her way out the front door, her blonde hair bouncing as she swayed her hips in that sensual way. She never walked like that, unless she was on the prowl for a good dicking. I chuckled under my breath, thanking my past self for shaving my legs, as I followed her out.

*

An hour later, I was two Blue Hawaiians deep and already feeling the buzz

18

when the door to the Craving Crab opened.

Davia gripped my arm in her hand, "That's Greg," she whispered, excitement practically oozing out of her pores. I followed the line of her gaze to the handsome man who had just entered the bar. His dark skin was on display under his completely unbuttoned short-sleeve button-down. He had a nice body, I guess, but it was early May and still cold…and he was wearing nearly nothing.

I turned to Davia, expecting to make a joke about his outfit, but she was practically drooling over him. I stifled a laugh.

I turned my attention back to the new arrival, he had spotted us and was making his way over in our direction, with a man trailing behind him. It wasn't until they were only a few feet from our table that I really got a good look at Greg's friend. Pale skin, sandy blonde hair, and blue eyes. He wore a dark blue polo and tan shorts. He looked like a frat boy on vacation. Which he probably was. He was decidedly, not even remotely, actually the farthest thing from my type. I tried to catch Davia's eyes to silently tell her I was going to kill her, but she was already out of her chair and flinging her arms around Greg's neck in a sensual hello.

I turned my murderous gaze from her and smiled at my date for the evening. His eyes were trailing my body appreciatively, something most girls loved, except I hated the way it made me feel to have his gaze on me. A vicious memory threatened to poke its way into the forefront of my mind, but I pushed it away.

"Hi, I'm Athena," I asserted over the music that filled the bar, extending my hand to him. The blonde boy took it in his own, and I felt his thumb rub a small circle on my skin, sending a shock through my body, and not the fun sexy kind, but the kind that had alarm bells going off.

I pulled my hand back, with some resistance. "I'm Louis, and you are hot as hell." Ugh, even his voice was a red flag. I fought against every fiber in my body that told me to grab my purse and run.

"Um, thanks," I replied, shifting awkwardly in my seat, casting a glance in Davia's direction. Davia and Greg had already locked faces in an incredibly graphic display of affection.

I was going to kill her.

"So, Athena, you look like you work out," Louis beamed, sitting down on the stool closest to me. I fought against the urge to kick it out from under him. Who the fuck says that to someone when you first meet them?

"I ride my bike everywhere," I answered bluntly, not wanting to give this kid anything.

"Yeah, you definitely have the rider's legs." I nearly choked on my drink as I turned back to him. He was not-so-subtly checking out my legs, the legs that stupid Davia forced me to have on display tonight.

"Ok," I gripped my glass and took a long drink, begging the pineapple rum to wash over my tongue and cover the bad taste of this date. It wasn't working.

Davia and Greg were all over each other for the next twenty minutes, she didn't even stop to introduce me. That man better have the best sex game in the world cause I'm never letting this bitch pull another 'vagina card' in her life.

I listened to Louis go on and on about his rugby team and their national title. Which would have been impressive had he not been trying to show me clips of his highlight film all night. I swear if I hear him say the word 'skirmish' one more time, I might ask them to hold everything other than rum in this next drink.

I was leaning my head on my palm, nodding with feigned excitement as Louis regaled the final three minutes of the 'most epic game ever' in excruciating detail when the door to the bar opened.

Framed in the dim orange light from the street lamps outside were four individuals. The moment my eyes caught a glimpse of their silhouettes I felt my breath catch in my throat. Tall and slender they slipped inside, the entire bar seemed to recognize their presence, like a cold chill of air traveling your spine. My hair stood on edge and goosebumps erupted over my entire body dancing along my skin like a sensual touch. The first individual in front had pale skin, nearly white, dark hollowed cheeks and a strong chiseled jawline. His honey-golden eyes were framed by dark circles, but he didn't look frightening. He looked strong. A kind of strength I found myself drawn to. His broad chest was covered in a black t-shirt, and he had an unbuttoned white jean jacket hugging his body. Dark black hair was pulled back and fastened in a bun at the nape of his neck. The ink from some tattoos threatened to poke out of the collar of his t-shirt and his ears and face were decorated with piercings. Dark jeans were tucked into tall black boots as he stepped inside.

Flanking him on his left was quite possibly the most stunning woman I had ever laid eyes on. Her silky black skin was blemish-free and nearly glowing. I watched her strong frame move across the floor with such grace that I wouldn't be surprised if she was royalty. Her long brown hair was braided into thick tresses, some were gathered at the top of her head in a thick cornet, while single strands fell down her back and onto her shoulders. Her lips were painted a bright candy apple red, the sinful color drew my eyes directly to her, and I felt myself licking my own lips in response.

On the other side of the man in the white jacket was a shorter individual wearing a grey button-down shirt, rolled up to the elbows. Their blonde hair was cropped short, just above their ears, hanging loosely across their tanned forehead. Their skin was a stunning tanned shade that looked like they received a healthy dose of sunshine, but could only really be achieved by lucky genetics. They, unlike the first two to enter the room, smiled warmly at those that they passed on their way to the table in the back corner. While the other two seemed to scream mystery, this one screamed comfort, but they were no less beautiful.

Bringing up the rear of the group was an imposing man, with marble-like skin that was pale and smooth. He had short black hair, slightly longer on the top than the sides, combed and slicked back. He wore an honest-to-god three-piece suit. The pants and jacket were a stunning blood-red color, and the vest had a golden design over a black button-down shirt unbuttoned to reveal the slim base of his throat.

I nearly lost the ability to breathe.

Who the hell are they? And why are they so fucking hot?

"Um, hottie alert," Davia whispered into my ear, the first thing she's said to me since her boy toy arrived, her mouth hanging open.

"Do you know them?" I asked back, vaguely aware of Louis still droning on about his game.

"If I did, do you think I'd be over here with you?" She joked. I couldn't pull my eyes from them as they took their seats in the corner booth. There was one singular red light above that booth and it cast an ominous glow over the drop-dead gorgeous newcomers. I was studying them, my heart beating quickly until the man in the suit turned his knowing gaze to me. His dark eyes looked nearly black from here and I felt a deep thrumming of my heartbeat in my chest and down below at my core, his eyes held mine and I felt the warmth pool between my legs. I don't know how long we sat there, staring at each other, but suddenly Louis moved his head until he was directly in my eye line. I ripped my eyes from the strangers for the first time since their arrival, my senses coming back to me in waves when I realized that Louis had asked me a question.

"I'm sorry, what?" He smiled, despite the annoyed look that flashed across his face.

"Do you need another drink?" Louis asked. On one hand, I really did want another drink, especially if I'm going to have to sit through another hour of Louis' company, on the other, I did not want this guy to think I owed him anything in return. He'd be lucky if he got a goodbye high-five from me tonight.

"I can get it, no worries," I started, beginning to slide off the stool. He put a hand on my thigh and I fought the impulse to slap it away.

"Allow me." He leaned in, his breath felt sticky and warm and smelled vaguely of Bud Light.

"No, it's ok. I can buy my own drinks." I pushed past him, trying not to be too obvious when I ripped my thigh from his grasp and made my way to the bar.

For the first time since Louis arrived, I felt like I could breathe. What was it about frat guys that made my skin crawl? Actually, I knew exactly what it was about that kind of guy that made me sick. These were the kind of guys who got everything they wanted, no matter what. Even if they had to take it. Davia knew my aversion to that type, and I better get like, unlimited favors from her for putting up with this tonight.

"Another?" Mike, the bartender asked. I nodded. Mike was a good friend of my mother's, but truth be told we hadn't spent much time together since her funeral. I appreciated how kind he was during that period of my life, but I had too much on my plate to try and maintain anything other than the business and my own sanity. A lot of relationships fell by the wayside.

"And you?" Mike asked, looking over my shoulder. I didn't have to turn to feel them there. The presence was thick, like honey. And just as tempting. I turned my head slightly to catch a glimpse of the sexy patron.

It was the pierced one. The one with the tattoos, and the hair, and the eyes… and the broad chest… and the strong hands…the one who… What was I saying?

"Four shots of bourbon," the man asserted, his voice a deep timber that nearly vibrated through my whole body. Oh god, yep, I'm definitely gonna need to use my toys tonight, I thought as I pressed my thighs together searching for some kind of relief.

"You got it," Mike replied, getting to work on our orders, leaving me alone with Mr. Tall, Dark, and Sinful. I suddenly forgot what to do with my arms. I first stuffed my hands into the pockets of my leather jacket but felt like my elbows were sticking out too far making me look like a chicken flapping its wings. Then, I leaned my forearms onto the bar in front of me, misjudging the distance and falling forward much further than I expected, which sent my ass jutting straight back as if in an open invitation. I stood up quickly with a groan under my breath. Did he see that? Did he like it?

I shook my head.

Get it together girl.

I risked one glance over my shoulder at the man, and found him staring directly at me, his honey eyes meeting my gaze with such an intensity that I wasn't sure I could look away if I wanted to.

We stood there, trapped in each other's gazes for what felt like far too long, and yet not quite long enough.

Fucking say something, don't just stare at him.

"Sup?"

The moment the meek word slipped through my lips, I stifled a whimper. Did I seriously just say, 'sup'?

If I could tear my gaze from his right now, I would facepalm.

He didn't respond, he didn't even flinch at my juvenile greeting. He just... watched me.

"Your drinks." Mike's voice drew the man's attention away, finally releasing me from his gaze. He slipped a twenty down on the counter, leaning in just enough so I could smell his woodsy scent, before gripping the shots and slinking away. I dropped a five on the counter and smiled at Mike before making my way back to my table with my drink. Avoiding looking at the table in the corner of the room.

I didn't want to look at Louis, and I definitely didn't want to look at that table, so I found myself staring at a poster of a shark holding a beer in its fin on the wall. Davia and Greg had vanished, probably to give each other those mind-blowing orgasms again.

I felt the faint buzz of my phone with a message from her.

DAVIA: Same address as yesterday, but if you hear screams, don't come knocking ;) Have fun!

ATHENA: I'm going to kill you.

DAVIA: love you! <3

I shook my head, seriously contemplating revoking her best friend card, I turned back to Louis and found him sitting even closer than he was before, his eyes studying my drink.

"So, it looks like it's just you and me now." His attempt at a sensual seductive tone came across as creepy, and I seriously wanted to leave, but I had just gotten a new drink and I wasn't going to let this creep keep me from enjoying it.

I grabbed the glass and took a few long sips.

"Yep, looks like it." I didn't allow myself another glance at the table in the corner, but I knew they were still there, their presence was fucking magnetic.

My third drink was hitting me harder than normal, either that or the sheer sexual prowess of these strangers had me in absolute shambles.

"You wanna get out of here?" Louis asked, his hand finding my thigh again. I went to brush his palm off of my skin but missed. My vision was blurring slightly. Shit, maybe I should have had more dinner.

"Actually, I am going to go home," I murmured, slowly standing, rocking off-balance on my feet.

Thank god I wore my Vans.

"Aww, come on, our friends are gonna be occupied for hours. You don't want to leave me with nowhere to go do you?" His lips brushed my cheek, and I felt bile rise in my throat, and my head swam. I couldn't focus on anything in my surroundings. I needed to get out of here.

"I'm going home. Alone." I heard the words slur despite my best attempt to keep them coherent. Something was wrong, and an eerie familiarity washed over me. I felt my entire body tighten in fear.

"I'll walk you," Louis offered, flinging an arm around my shoulders and leading me out the front door. I don't remember the walk from the table to the street outside, but as soon as I felt the cool night air hit my clammy skin, I knew I needed to vomit. I rushed to the alley where the dumpster was, and puked up the contents of my stomach. My lips were chapped, my mouth was dry, and my chest felt heavy.

Tears pooled in my eyes as my mind struggled to remain clear.

"Come on baby, let me take care of you." I felt Louis' hands gripping my hips from behind as I was bent over, his erection pressed against my ass.

No. No. No. NO. Please. Not again.

"Leave me alone," I cried, but the words weren't there. "Please, go away." My pleas were nothing more than grunts.

"Don't worry, it'll feel really good." The cold air hit my ass cheeks as my dress was pushed up around my hips exposing my thong. I tried to break free from his grasp but his strength felt insurmountable in my current state. I felt the hot tears spill down my cheeks. Memories slammed into my chest. Rough hands. The static of the radio. Whiskey. The senses of my nightmares.

"Stop. Hel-" They weren't fully formed, but I mustered every ounce of energy I had left to scream, but my shout was cut short by a slap across my face. The sting felt like it traveled down my spine as my head snapped back. I tasted blood.

I heard the tell-tale sound of a zipper and I tried to pull myself from him one more time. I had been a victim before, and I barely survived. I don't think I would be so 'lucky' if it were to happen again.

"Don't fucking move, you teasing bitch," he hissed through gritted teeth. "You wear this tight ass dress, showing off your fucking cleavage all night, and you don't give me the time of fucking day?" I whimpered, trying to pull from his grip as he pulled my thong to the side. I felt his bare cock notch against my entrance.

There was nothing I could do.

I screamed and pounded against the brick wall in front of me with every ounce of dwindling energy I had left. Hitting the bricks as if they were *him*. The monster from my nightmares.

Then I felt his vicious presence dissipate as he was pulled away from me. I didn't have the energy to stand on my own without his selfish hands holding me up, a sickening dilemma, but before I fell to the ground, a pair of hands caught me.

"Let me go, you fuckers!" I heard Louis exclaim. I couldn't see a thing, the world was tilting on its axis as whatever drug he fed me took over my senses.

I faintly heard the sounds of flesh hitting flesh, grunts of fighting, and groans of pain.

"You're going to wish you never fucking touched her," I heard a voice whisper. It was threatening, dominant, and calm, like a viper poised to attack.

"Fuck you!" Louis cried, but his tone was laced with fear. "Wait, what the hell are you?!"

Good.

I want him to be afraid.

I want him to suffer.

"Get her out of here," the dominant voice said. The arms that were holding me in place reached around so they could gather and lift me until I was settled in against their arms. Instinctively I laid my head against their chest, cold and hard, like tile flooring. I knew I should be afraid, worried that I traded one threat for another. But something about the grip on my body, the caring way they wiped my hair from my forehead, I knew I could trust this savior.

"Fuck, she's bleeding," an accented voice said. I felt the arms around me tense, as their face leaned closer to mine. I felt their cold breath against my lips. I willed my eyes to open, but the lids were too heavy.

"Control yourself, Laz." A feminine command.

I felt blackness slowly closing in on my consciousness when I felt the figure's face lean close to mine until our lips were mere inches apart. I wasn't afraid of being claimed unwillingly again though, something about this presence felt safe. Secure.

"Oh, shit…" The figure exclaimed, fear, wonder, and something else entirely laced their tone.

And then it all went dark.

ORPHEUS

TWO

"Are you sure we can't stay here longer than tonight?" Silas asked, sliding into our booth with four shots of bourbon in his hands. I didn't justify his stupid question with an answer, instead, I reached across the table and gripped my shot glass in hand.

"You got your eye on someone?" Samara teased, her red lips pursed to plant an air kiss. Silas elbowed her and she coughed, devolving into laughter.

"The redhead with the short-as-sin dress on." He nodded his head in her direction. Both Samara and Laz turned to look, but I refrained because I already knew what I would see. I'd gotten a nice look when we first arrived. As my companions ogled over the busty redhead, I fixed the lapel of my suit jacket.

"I could smell her arousal the moment we walked into the room," Laz whispered in a soft southern accent, licking their lips.

"I wonder what her blood smells like," Samara added. The three of them looked like a pack of ravenous monsters ready to devour their prey. Which, I guess they were.

"You know we cannot hunt in this area," I said, drawing their attention back to me. My Romanian accent was not as thick as it used to be, it's been nearly a century since I've returned, and time will dilute a lot of things.

"Who said anything about hunting her?" Silas tossed toward me, leaning back into the booth and letting his tongue run over his lip piercing. "I just want a taste." I saw the gleam in his eyes and barely stopped myself from groaning.

"You cannot feed on anyone in this town, Silas." It wasn't often that I went full coven leader on my companions. Oh who am I kidding…it's daily that I need to go full coven leader on them. The hungry, horny bastards are always getting into trouble. "Need I remind you that your hunger and libido are the reason we are on the run in the first place?"

That got his attention, finally drawing his gaze from the nameless redhead.

"You had your fair share if I remember correctly." Silas tossed back, an edge of anger in their voice. My mind flooded back to that night. The gilded mansion, the sensual offerings, the trap.

"Stop, both of you," Samara scolded, casually leaning back in the booth. "We all made mistakes, which is why we all made the choice to go on the move." It wasn't exactly a choice, but she was right, we all contributed to our current predicament. A mistake I will not be letting us make again.

"I do not like the way that guy is looking at her though," Laz responded under their breath. I'd noticed the blonde boy sitting entirely too close to her when we first arrived. He seemed so caught up in himself that he didn't notice his date was practically drooling as we entered.

She wasn't the only one.

"Yeah, that guy gives me the creeps. Do you see the way he's got his hand on her thigh?" Silas was back to looking at the mystery woman. I rolled my eyes.

"Can we stop talking about the girl and take our shots?" I exclaimed, exasperated.

Samara gripped her glass and raised it above her head. "To fresh starts." To her credit, she was a hopelessly optimistic soul. She saw our life on the run as a new beginning, and every time we picked up what little roots we managed to plant in one place and rushed to a new chapter, she saw it as an opportunity. I wondered how long that unbridled optimism might last. Or if she was truly just masking the pain we all knew she'd been feeling since we were held captive.

"To finally feeding soon," Silas teased, but I knew he wasn't joking, we had been very careful not to feed for the last three stops, and it wasn't going to be easy to resist much longer. But we had a plan and feeding in this small town where everyone knows everyone was not a part of it.

"To The Wanderers," Laz contributed, lifting their shot glass over their head. We'd been known as The Wanderers Coven long before our nomadic new life, but now it fits even more than it had then.

"To surviving," I added, then the four of us tossed our drinks back letting the warm amber liquid warm our cold, dead insides.

"Hey, what the fuck?" Silas exclaimed. I followed his gaze, although I didn't need to. He was clearly looking at the redhead. She was stumbling out of her stool, and the bumbling idiot beside her was gripping her exposed skin possessively. A growl rumbled in my chest.

"Leave it be," I bristled, matter-of-factly.

"She doesn't look good," Samara mused, sitting a bit straighter in her seat. Her fangs elongated slightly as she watched the couple.

"She's been drinking, she's fine. Leave it be," I repeated, adding an edge of authority to my voice. Her fangs retracted.

I heard the door open and close and knew that the pair had made their way outside. Hopefully, now my coven could focus on something else.

Silas was out of his seat immediately, crossing the bar to her vacated table. I rolled my eyes, and let my forehead fall into my hand.

Silas returned with her half-drank drink in his hands, slipping back into the booth he put the blue liquid down in front of him.

"Laz?" He said, sliding it across the table to them. Laz had the unique ability to discern the contents of any mixture. It kept us from drinking poisoned blood on more than one occasion. You can never be too careful with Hunters on your tail.

Laz gripped the drink and pulled it to their nose, inhaling deeply. Their eyes fell closed as they analyzed the drink in front of them. I eagerly awaited the moment that they put everyone's fears to rest and we could get on with our evening. I was looking forward to at least two more shots before we found our way to the inn.

No such luck.

Laz's eyes sprang open revealing the telltale sign of a near shift, bloodshot eyes, and red rims. Their fangs elongated and I quickly leaned forward to block their frame from anyone in the bar.

"It's drugged," Laz hissed in an almost violent manner, and suddenly all hell was breaking loose. Samara's sharpened fingernails dug into the table top and Silas sprung up out of his seat.

"Stop, now. All of you. Calm yourselves." I whispered with as much authority as I could. They turned to look at me, of course, they did. I was their leader. My heart remained calm. One beat every hour, that's all we got now. The result of our suspended animation. A reminder of the half-life we now led.

"She needs our help," Silas spoke through clenched teeth, his features had not shifted yet, but I knew he was nearly on the verge.

"Ground rules. She doesn't see you shifted, and he doesn't die." It was clear they wouldn't put this behind them without doing something, but at least we could stick to the plan. They nodded, tense. I stood calmly and led them out of the bar, keeping Laz close behind me. They had the good sense to keep their eyes tilted downward and their mouth shut as we walked past the remaining patrons.

I felt her fear the moment we were outside. It gripped my senses with a violent hold. Nearly inescapable. Her muffled cries of pain sent us all into action. Quick on our feet, we rounded the corner to the alley beside the bar. The sight in front of me was one I would never forget. Even if I tried.

The redheaded woman was braced against the brick wall next to the dumpster, her dress bunched around her waist, her underwear ripped to the side as this man stood behind her, ready to take from her what did not belong to him.

I saw red. I knew I had shifted, feeling the tell-tale prick of my fangs against my bottom lip as I wrapped my fingers across this bastard's neck and pulled him back. I felt my elongated and pointed nails dig into his flesh, and it took every ounce of self-restraint to keep from ripping his spine out through his neck and feeding it to him.

I was vaguely aware of Laz catching the small-framed woman before she fell to the ground, their eyes scanning her for injuries before carefully pulling her dress down to cover her. Her fear was consuming me, flooding my senses to the point where I could barely feel anything else. Not the cool night air, not the trembling of the man in my clutches. It was her and her terror. I'd never felt fear so poignant. If my blood wasn't perpetually chilled, it'd be boiling.

Silas joined me in restraining the asshole. Before I could stop him, his fist connected with the man's jaw. I held him in place as Silas landed another hit to his gut.

"Let me go, you fuckers!" The vile creature hissed. I caught a glimpse of the bruise that was already darkening on the redhead's face. I leaned my lips close to this asshole's ear, and calmly uttered, "You're going to wish you never fucking touched her." It was a miracle that I could restrain myself from screaming at this man, truthfully. But I wanted my privacy in order to punish him the way he deserved. To make him suffer.

"Fuck you!" He spat. Silas landed another punch on his ribs, I heard one crack. Silas' control slipped and I saw his eyes go red, his fangs sharpening as he stalked toward his prey. Shit. "Wait, what the hell are you?!" Fuck. He had seen us. We had been careless. There was only one way out of this now. I had to make another plan, and quickly.

"Get her out of here," I ordered Laz. They nodded, bending down to gather the woman in their arms. Then I saw it, deep crimson blood marring her stunning face.

"Fuck, she's bleeding." Laz's mouth fell open and their fangs begged for the chance to sink into this woman's life force. Hell, I was all the way over here and I still wanted a taste. This was not good. Her scent wasn't strong though. It smelled wrong, almost toxic. A blessing in disguise, because I'm not sure any of us would have been able to control ourselves with the already unsteady hold on our monsters had she smelled as good as I thought she would.

"Control yourself, Laz," Samara voiced calmly. She was the only one of the three of us who had yet to shift, sometimes her restraint truly surprised me.

Silas took hold of the writhing wannabe rapist in my hands and held a tight grip around his throat, keeping him from crying out. I felt my features return to normal, the red tint that the world had a moment ago slipped away as the cloud of anger cleared. But her fear was still there. Still gnawing at me. Everyone else? They were angry. I felt their anger burning violently, spurring me on.

"Oh, shit…" I turned to see Laz taking a deep inhale of the woman's scent, and I readied myself to jump in, to keep them from creating a second body we'd have to worry about tonight because there was no way this douche was surviving the next ten minutes. But instead, their features reverted, their eyes cleared and their fangs retracted. Shock colored their expression and filled the air around me. I didn't have time to analyze it or ask.

"Follow her scent, get her to her home, safely." Laz nodded, acknowledging that they had heard me, but didn't take their eyes from the woman in their arms.

"Samara, go with them. Nothing happens to her, do you understand?" Samara nodded, and I watched the two of them take off into the night, the woman's crimson hair swaying with every step Laz took.

When I turned back to the blonde whimpering mess, I was pleased to see that he hadn't passed out yet. If I was going to kill him, I wanted him to experience every ounce of pain I was going to put him through.

"There's a camera in front of the bar. You know what to do, Silas." He loosened his hold on the asshole's neck, and I watched in awe as my companion transformed. As often as I'd seen Silas' gift in action, it still amazed me. A moment later I was looking at two identical figures. Silas' form was now a completely accurate mirror for the fucker in my hands.

"What the hell?!" The man whimpered weakly, his voice strained from the crushing hold I had on his neck.

"You deserve to rot in hell," Silas spat in his face before taking off toward the front of the bar to lead the trail in the complete opposite direction. He was good at what he did. He would make sure at least a dozen cameras saw him walking home alone. Doorbell cameras, businesses, he might even step inside a gas station for a quick look around.

Having Silas and his ability was one of the main assets that have helped us hide the way we had for so long.

Knowing that we were taken care of as far as an alibi, I turned my attention back to the worthless creature in front of me.

"I normally don't drink spoiled blood," I taunted, stalking forward, letting my vision redden, and opening my mouth to display my growing fangs. "But for you, I'll make an exception."

He wanted to scream, but I didn't give him the chance.

LAZ

THREE

My entire body was on fire, like the very venom in my veins was eating me alive. My skin felt electrified where her body met mine. She was so petite. So vulnerable. The mere thought of what that man was about to do to her nearly sent me tumbling down a hole of lost control.

It was the scent of her blood that calmed me though, ironically. Her face was caked with it, and I saw the bruise beginning on her skin. I hope Orpheus and Silas made his death hurt. Her blood was so tainted by the drug that he had slipped her that I couldn't even get a smell of the *real* her beneath it all. Anger was the only thing I could feel.

There are many out there in the world that would call me the monster, but how am *I* the one they fear when men like him exist? It sickens me to my very core.

"Her scent leads this way." Samara ran beside me, her face stoic and calm. She always was the best in a crisis. I followed the direction she led us, holding this beautiful woman tight to my chest. Beneath the blood that was drying on her ivory skin, I could see her features. She had dark-painted lips, and her eyelids were first arrived at the bar. Of course, I noticed. Her long red ponytail was silky, and smooth and smelled like wintergreen as her head lulled against my chest.

She was breathing steadily, but I was worried about the effect of the drug on her system.

"Can you do something for her?" I asked as Samara turned down a gravel driveway. We ran quietly, our footsteps barely registering on the rocky ground.

"Once we get her inside, I'll do what I can." I nodded, although Samara wasn't looking at me. We quickly arrived at a quaint blue cottage. I don't know anything about this woman, but somehow this home made perfect sense. It felt like her.

Which I understand was entirely ridiculous to say, but it's true. I hugged her tighter to my body as Samara gripped a set of keys from the purse in her hand.

I hadn't even noticed that she picked up the girl's purse. That's why I loved having Samara in our coven, she was detail-oriented. Orpheus saw the big picture, Silas and I were good at executing plans, but Samara never let things fall through the cracks. She unlocked the door and pushed it open, but then stopped just in front of the threshold.

"Shit," she exclaimed. Damn, this was going to prove to be an issue.

"Hey. You need to invite us inside." I caressed the side of her bruising face. Her brows furrowed as she stirred in my arms. "That's it, wake up." She groaned, her arms moving slightly. "Can we go inside your house?" I asked, calmly, and quietly. Then she nodded. My heart thumped in my chest.

"She's gotta say the words, Laz."

"I know that," I snapped. "Hey there, Darlin'. I need you to say something for me." She groaned again and I gently shook her in my arms.

"Darlin'?" Samara asked, teasingly.

Ignoring her, I gripped the woman's small frame and whispered in her ear.

"Tell me I can come in," I cooed in my silky southern accent. The slightest whimper escaped her mouth and I felt my length strain against my pants immediately. "Please."

"Come in," she mumbled against my chest. The words were no more than a jumbled gargled mess, but they were enough.

Samara cautiously stepped one foot through the door, and a sigh of relief flooded me. "Thank you," I whispered to my sleeping beauty as I stepped inside. The inside of her home was even more perfect than the outside. With cozy colorful furniture and bright abstract art decorating the walls this home felt lived-in, in the most comfortable sense of the word. A table with a baby blue record player sat against one of the walls. Several records were filed neatly on the shelves underneath it. I followed Samara into a room, the girl's bedroom clearly, based on the saturation of her minty scent. A king-sized bed took up much of the space, but the walls again were decorated with bright lively images. My eye, however, was immediately drawn to the bookshelf. Hundreds of titles, ranging from fiction to non-fiction, fantasy to drama. I snickered at the copy of Twilight that sat on her bottom shelf before moving to place her down on the center of the mattress. It wasn't lost on me the immediate sense of emptiness I felt the moment she was out of my arms.

"Should we change her?" I asked, glancing down at her dress, a few drops of blood had landed on the front of the purple fabric, and I wanted nothing more than to burn it so that she never had to relive what happened to her tonight.

"No, she needs to think she got drunk and came home to pass out," I growled at her words.

"She needs to know what happened to her tonight," I argued. She needs to know that he didn't violate her.

"Orpheus won't want us to get involved." She waved me off.

Get involved? The thought made me laugh. Somehow I was already so deeply involved that I was furious with the prospect of her not knowing the truth.

I opened my mouth to respond but Samara had already taken her place on her knees near the woman's face. She leaned in, letting her eyes drift closed as she sent her ability out.

I watched carefully as she worked, her palms gracing the skin of the woman's perfect face. Samara was one of the best healers our kind has ever seen. If there was anything physically wrong with the sleeping angel, she would be able to fix it. It's the mental scars from tonight that she would have to find a way to live with.

I felt my fists tighten at my side as the memory of that man behind her as she cried out for help returned to me.

I had half a mind to go find Orpheus and Silas right now to make sure that they made him pay. To ensure that they are dragging out his torture in the most deviant and violent way possible. But I knew they would.

I trusted them to avenge her.

"She'll be fine," Samra said, rising from her knees. Her index finger trailed along the woman's face and I watched as the bruise that was darkening on the woman's face slowly dissolved.

We had almost picked a different bar. There's another town about thirty minutes away with another joint. Had we made our way there instead we wouldn't have been here. We wouldn't have been able to stop him. She would have - "I'm glad we were here," I lamented, not liking the train of thought that my mind was taking. Samara simply nodded, her eyes remaining on the girl before us.

"I don't want to leave her just yet," I claimed, truthfully. A little ashamed at how attached I had grown to this human already.

"Me either," Samara responded and I found myself breathing steadily again. Nodding, I took a seat on the far end of the mattress. I was careful not to let it dip too much under my weight.

Samara sank to the floor at the foot of the bed, her back up against the wall.

"Her blood feels wrong," Samara whispered after a while, her brow furrowing. I sighed deeply. "I helped as much as I could."

"It's got a lot of that drug in it." I thought back to the drink we left on our table. The blue drink she had been sipping on. If she only drank half of it and reacted like this, I shuddered to think of how the whole glass might have affected her.

"She could have died." Samara was only stating what I already knew. The question was, why did we care so much? It is not that we don't care about humans…ok well, we really don't. We only care enough to find the vilest of humans, the ones who deserve to die. But we all jumped to her rescue tonight. Each of us.

"I know."

We sat in comfortable silence for an hour, watching over our little human, listening to her steady breathing and watching her chest rise and fall until our phones buzzed.

ORPHEUS: It's done. Meet me at the inn.

A weight lifted from my chest. The world would be a better place without that scum in it. But then a different weight landed squarely on my shoulders. "I don't want to leave her all alone here," I explained as Samara and I stood from our seats.

"We can't watch her forever."

I knew she was right, so why did a part of me want to believe that we could?

SILAS

FOUR

"Tell me again," I hissed at Orpheus as we sat in our motel room. The dingy floors and ugly wallpaper were a constant, annoying reminder that we were on the run and that the comfort and luxury that we had grown so accustomed to over our centuries of life was not only a thing of the past, but also the one thing that could get us killed. For real this time. I caught a glimpse of my reflection in a large square mirror that was mounted on the wall. Taking in my large frame, dark hair, ink, and piercings, I was thankful that I was myself again. I hadn't felt as skeevy in someone else's form as I did tonight in a while. That tool had it coming. And I for one, was glad I'll never have to wear his face again.

"I ripped out his throat, drained him completely and once I knew he was long dead, I relieved his body of his head and tossed the pieces of him out to sea," Orpheus explained nonchalantly, as if he wasn't describing the brutal way in which he murdered a man tonight. He leaned back in the armchair, resting his ankle on his knee. His red suit was still pristine. How he managed to feed and keep his suit clear was beyond me.

"Did you save any?" I wasn't starving right now, but I knew that soon we would be and if we already hunted in this city we might as well make the most of it.

"Of course, I did." Orpheus nodded to the mini fridge that sat in the corner of the room. I sauntered over and pushed open the door. The rush of air felt warm against my already cold skin as I looked inside. Six plastic water bottles sat side by side, filled to the brim with dark crimson blood. I licked my lips at the sight. It had been too long since our last hunt.

I gripped one in my hand and smiled at the feeling of it in my hand, still warm.

"Drink up, Silas." Orpheus didn't smile, but he had a damn good smirk that really only showed itself when things went according to plan, or he just completed a particularly great hunt.

And considering all of our plans went completely to hell tonight, I'd assume he enjoyed tearing that asshole to pieces. I'd take the smirk over his bitching any day.

The first sip of the still warm blood had me groaning, an intoxicating heat and rush of pleasure bloomed in my chest. Drinking blood was an almost euphoric activity. It's why so many vampires feed during sex. But blood from the bottle, even fresh blood like this, didn't have the same effect that drinking directly from the vein did.

I swallowed down the whole bottle in seconds, and then when it was empty, I licked my lips and the tips of my elongated fangs to savor the flavor. I always forgot how dimmer and duller the world looked and felt when I was hungry. When I had fresh blood in my system it was like the entire world lit up like a damn Christmas tree.

All my senses were sharper, including my hearing, which is why I could tell that Laz and Samara were going to walk through the door in 5…4…3…2….

"I smell blood," Laz crowed the moment they crossed the threshold. I laughed, my large frame shaking as I leaned down and opened the fridge door again.

Laz moved quickly, grabbing a bottle and downing it in seconds. Samara was slightly more reserved than that. She always was. But she indulged all the same.

"I trust you had no issue getting the human back to her home?" Orpheus asked, business as always. He was seriously killing my blood buzz. Although I would be lying if I didn't admit I was also interested in how the human was doing.

"She's safe and sound," Laz replied. I found myself feeling strangely relieved at that notion. I still didn't quite understand my reaction to the thought of her in danger. Sure, I hated men like that, and we've hunted men for doing less, but the fact that it was her that was threatened. The sexy redhead who got all flustered around me. The one whose arousal I could smell the moment she realized it was me who was standing behind her at the bar. I nearly dropped to my knees to have a taste right there.

Then to see what that asshole was going to do to her? Trying to steal her arousal, the wetness that was entirely for my sake, and rape her? Anger began bubbling under the surface again and I bit down on my lip, struggling against the impulse to go find his rotting corpse and set it on fire so he suffers, even in hell.

Why do I care that much?

"We need to leave first thing tomorrow." All of our heads turned to look at Orpheus, who was standing slowly and removing his suit jacket. "Get a few hours of rest and we will leave before the sun comes up."

"You want us to travel during the day?" Samara asked, incredulous. It was a fair question. Although we had completed the necessary rituals to survive being in sunlight, it still wasn't a pleasant feeling. Like a bad sunburn. Compared to a fiery combustible death though, it was a walk in the park.

"The sooner we leave this town the better."

I felt the attitude in the room shift. Almost imperceptible, but it was there.

"I can't leave until I know she's ok," Laz spoke first.

"I agree," Samara added. Orpheus ran a hand down his face.

"You said she was safe and sound, what more do you want?" He was holding on to the last thread of his control. If there was one thing Orpheus hated, it was feeling out of control, and right now nothing was going according to his plan.

"I don't want to leave yet, either," I found myself agreeing aloud and Orpheus tossed his hands in the air above his head.

"You're all ridiculous, why are you all suddenly so obsessed with this damn human?" I didn't know the answer to that, but I was interested in finding out.

When none of us answered, he growled, low and threatening. He could be a terrifying creature when he wanted to be.

"Fucking fine," he said, giving in. I smiled at the prospect of seeing my sexy little redhead again. "One day. That's all."

I only hoped that would be enough time to satisfy this strange desire.

ATHENA

NINE

The sunlight peeking through the blinds of my bedroom warmly embraced my face and I instinctively moved to shield myself from its brightness. Cool leather touched my forehead as I brought my arm to my eyes. Then I bolted out of bed, the rush of last night coming back to me in silent dreadful waves.

The bar. The outfit. Davia. Greg. Louis.

My stomach churned at the thought of his name.

Other than the fact that I was wearing the same dress from last night, with no idea how I made it back home, I feel fine. There's no blinding headache, dry mouth, or nausea that usually accompanies a morning after an evening spent at the Craving Crab, taunting me.

Ok, what the hell happened last night?

How did I get here?

What happened with Louis?

I slid off of my bed and padded carefully to the bathroom, my hair was ratted, falling from the ponytail it was confined to, and my dress was rumpled, but that wasn't what had my jaw dropping. It was the cracked red blood that was caked around my nose, and a spot on my lip. I couldn't see an injury beneath the blood for the life of me, so how did it get there?

I felt my foundation shift uneasily, as I stared at my reflection in the harsh white light of my bathroom. Memories swam around my mind like out-of-order puzzle pieces.

Louis and I were talking. Davia and Greg had left. I got another drink. Those sexy-as-sin strangers arrived. And then…

I struggled to wade through the muddled memories of last night, attempting to reform the picture from the hazy clues. My drink. There was something wrong with my drink. Did I leave? Did I come home alone? That thought had me sprinting from my bathroom to search my tiny cottage for any signs of visitors last night.

Please, god, don't let Louis be here.

Much to my relief, I found no signs that anyone was currently or had recently been in my home. With that fear settled, I lumbered to the kitchen to make myself a cup of coffee.

As the glorious sounds of brewing coffee filled my ears, I rushed to find wherever I had discarded my phone last night. Maybe Davia would have some answers.

It was only nine in the morning. The bright picture of my Grandma and I sitting in one of the booths at The Maine Plotline flashed up at me from my lock screen. I had three unread messages. One from last night and two from early this morning.

DAVIA: Hey you minx, heard you left the bar with Louis. (Mike told me) Hope you have fun ;) I am three orgasms in, and we're recharging before the next round. Love you!

DAVIA: Good morning! Louis never came back to the rental last night so you must have had a great night. Can't wait to hear all the sweaty details. 8=====D ;)

A vicious throb began in my head as I read her first two texts. Did we leave the bar together? He never went home? None of the puzzle pieces were matching up.

DAVIA: Hey girl, Greg is trying to get ahold of Louis, can you have him call? They were supposed to meet up at 8.

My mind was moving a mile a minute. Bits and pieces of things were fighting their way back into my conscious mind. Nothing was clear, but I do remember one thing. One overwhelming emotion. Fear.

As I poured my coffee, I called Davia.

"Good morning sex kitten! Did you get my texts?" She answered, cheerfully. I shook my head.

"Davia, I didn't have sex last night." I was still trying to figure out what happened, but it had been so long since I had had sex, that I feel like if I did, I would be feeling it. Although I also should be feeling the alcohol and I felt perfectly fine.

"So what, you just talked all night? Jeez Athena, what a waste of good dick." She had a kind of subtle sexy morning voice that sounded almost sing-songy. It was a pleasant sound, except when it wasn't making any sense.

"No, I came home alone," I explained, hoping that the more I said it, the more it would feel like the truth.

"But Mike said you left together…" she started, but a deep call from the other side of the line cut her off.

"Is that Louis?" The owner of the voice was clearly annoyed, and it didn't escape me that this was the first time that I had actually heard him speak. Considering he never introduced himself last night, and he spent what little time he and Davia remained at the bar whispering naughty words into her willing and eager ears.

"No, just Athena. She says Louis never went home with her," I listened intently to what Greg would say to that.

"I thought you said they were together?" An edge of worry seeped into his tone.

"I thought they were." I could practically hear her shrug with indifference.

"Davia, can you meet me for breakfast?" I asked, hurriedly. If anyone could help me make sense of last night, it was her. As hard as I tried to keep the uncertainty and worry from my voice, I don't think I was successful. Somewhere deep in my mind, I felt the past threatening to resurface. Panic started to seize my heart, a lump forming in my throat.

"Sure, Dale's in twenty work for you?" My best friend was many things, impulsive, yes, sensual, definitely. Infuriating, most times. But supportive when she knew I needed her, always.

"See you there."

After hanging up, I took deep breaths and quickly cleaned last night's makeup and the mystery blood from my face. There were answers as to what happened last night somewhere. I needed to find them before I fell over the edge and the lock on my worst memories was broken. Maybe I needed to talk to Louis. As unfortunate as that thought was. It did seem like it was the best of my options. There were two people who left that bar last night, and one of them had no idea what the hell happened.

I tossed on my Shockgrove Community College sweater that Davia so rudely, and not at all sexily, ripped from my body last night. Pulling on a pair of soft black leggings and sliding my feet back into my Vans, I was ready to go.

Dale's was only a three-minute bike ride from my cottage. In fact, most of the town was within a ten-minute bike ride. That's why I never bothered learning to drive or getting a car. If I needed to leave the town, which I rarely did, Davia would take me, or I'd hop on the bus line.

As much as I hated it, as much as I loathed the idea of being trapped here, this town was my home. My entire existence. And I guess knowing every square inch of your hometown has its benefits. For example, I knew the secret path to a private beach area that I would take when I needed a few uninterrupted hours of thinking or reading. I knew the soft spot in the fence surrounding the lighthouse that would bend just enough for someone to slip through. I knew about the place just beneath the main pier that if you sat there at sunset you'd have a perfect view of the golden rays peeking out over the blue ocean. I knew this town back and forth, and while at times it felt stifling, it was a comforting pressure.

Dale's was packed, as it usually was this early on a Sunday morning. I locked my bike up and hurried inside to find Davia already seated. She waved me over, and I smiled, noticing that she was wearing the same outfit from last night, but had adorned Greg's button-down shirt over top.

"I ordered you a coffee." She pointed to the steaming ceramic cup sitting in front of the open chair. Thankfully, she let me take a full sip before she bombarded me with the questions I knew she was dying to ask.

"So, what the hell happened last night?" I sighed, trying to gather my still-jumbled thoughts.

"Truthfully, I don't know." It wasn't the best answer, but it was the one I had.

"What do you mean?" She wrapped her hands around her own cup and took a deep sip, patiently waiting for me to make sense. I wish I could.

"I went to the bar to get a drink-"

"And that hot tattooed guy was right behind you," she added.

"Oh, so you were paying attention to something other than Greg's mouth." She shrugged, unashamed. "Yes, he was there and I was being awkward as I am oft to do, then he left because he couldn't seem to get away fast enough." Damn, just the image of that broad-chested, long-haired masterpiece had me feeling tightness in my core. I wonder what that piercing on his lip would feel like as he licked my-

"Ok, but what about Louis, what happened with him?" Davia's question snapped me out of my panty-wetting daydream.

"Right, so I got my drink and went back to the table. That's when I saw you were gone. By the way, thanks for saying goodbye, bitch." She leaned back in her chair with a satisfied grin.

"I mean, we could have stayed but then you would have been getting a show."

I laughed with my friend, but it felt hollow. The question of what happened still loomed over me.

"So, Louis was talking and I was trying to figure out how to leave politely 'cause frankly, I've talked to brick walls that were more interesting than he was." Davia choked on her coffee, her hand came up to catch some drips as they sputtered from her mouth. "But that's where things start to get fuzzy."

"Fuzzy?" She asked as she wiped her face with a napkin.

"I don't know, I remember saying I wanted to go home. Louis told me he'd walk me. I said no. Then… nothing."

She stared at me for a long moment, her brows furrowing.

"Nothing?"

"Nothing until I woke up, alone in bed. Still dressed in last night's outfit. And-" I hesitated. I had theories about what happened in my lost time last night. It wasn't the first time, I'd lost time. Wasn't the first time I'd woken up with blood caked on my body. The feeling of fear. But did I want to worry her if it didn't even happen?

"And…" she prompted.

Taking a deep breath to steady myself, I continued. "And I had blood on my face. It looked like I may have had a bloody lip and nose last night." I saw her eyes dart to my features, quickly scanning to see if there were any obvious signs of injury.

"You're kidding me?" I knew she didn't think I was actually kidding her, but I could see the same theories I had beginning to form in her mind. Her face dropped.

"I don't know what happened, Davia. But I - nobody was in my house. It was locked and I didn't feel like I had… like I was… I don't think anyone touched me last night." I was rambling, it felt awful putting my fears into words rather than fleeting thoughts.

"Mike said he saw you two leave together. Oh my god, Athena. I'm so sorry. If that asshole drugged you, I'm going to fucking castrate him." Her eyes were burning, so honestly, I believed her.

"I just wish I knew what happened, it doesn't make any sense. These blank spots in my memory certainly feel like I was drugged, again. But I would be feeling the effects today if I were. I honestly feel fine." Fine is probably not the right word for it, but it was the one I was choosing to use at this moment.

A slight chill brushed against my neck as the door to the diner opened, a small chime sounding from the bell above the entry. I didn't turn to see the newcomers, but I felt a familiar presence that sent goosebumps erupting across my skin.

"Oh damn," Davia exclaimed, looking over my shoulder.

"It's them, isn't it? The group from the bar?" I knew the answer already, something about the air when they were around felt electric, like every molecule in the room chilled.

"Yeah, and fuck they look even hotter today if you can believe it." I couldn't. There was hardly anything they could improve upon their appearance from last night. "Wait, they were there last night!" She nearly jumped up out of her seat as the thought solidified to her. "They might have seen something. Or at least they can confirm if you actually left with Louis." It wasn't a bad idea. In fact, it was probably the best shot I had of figuring out what happened. But the thought of approaching them, trying to speak coherently in their presence, yeah I might have better luck just trying to remember on my own.

"Go ask them," Davia encouraged, using her hands to shoo me. I shook my head.

"I can't. That's so weird." I suddenly hated my choice of outfit, and the very bare makeup look I had done. My hair was pulled back in a claw clip, and if I had to face those insanely attractive people looking like this, I may die of embarrassment. "What do I say, like 'Hi, I know you were at the bar last night, did you happen to see if that dude I was with drugged me?'" Davia winced at my blunt words. I knew she probably felt a twinge of guilt at the whole thing, being the reason I was even out last night. But it was not her fault or her responsibility if that man was a monster. She also knew my history. She understood why this question was so painful to have unanswered.

"Do you wanna know what happened or not?" She pursed her lips and I knew she was right. They were there, there are four of them so chances are they might have seen something. Even the smallest bit of info might help me fill in these gaps that feel so volatile. To keep my mind from filling in the blanks with snapshots of my past, of *his* hands on my skin as he held me down. Of the feel of him inside of me as I cried out for help. I shook my head, forcing the image of his eyes back into the box I crafted for him a long time ago. If he was always going to be a part of me, the least he could do was remain locked away inside.

"I look horrible," I whined, gesturing to the 'everything' about me.

Davia reached across the table, pulling the claw clip from my head and allowing my red tresses to fall down across my shoulders. She ran her fingers through it a few times, trying to achieve the sexy bedhead vibe. She pinched my cheeks, bringing a faux blush to them. She leaned back in her chair and admired her work.

"So?" She smiled.

"You look hot, now go over there and see if they saw anything." I nodded awkwardly a few times before moving. By the time I was out of my chair, I felt my heart racing to an unhealthy degree. Only then did I turn to face their table.

It took only a second for me to realize that Davia was right. They *were* hotter today. The tattooed man who I accosted with the word 'sup' last night was wearing a tight white t-shirt over ripped black jeans. A jean jacket slung over the back of his booth. His arms were on display and his delicious-looking pale skin was decorated entirely in stunning black designs. From his fingers up until they disappeared under the sleeve of his shirt.

His hair that was pulled back at the nape of his neck last night was half up, half down, and a few wayward pieces hung haphazardly around his face, framing him like the work of art he was.

The shorter individual had their shaggy blonde hair slicked back, thick waves sitting against their neck. They had a black button-down tucked into jeans, and their soft eyes looked tired.

The woman was wearing a red sundress, and a black jean jacket, her hair flowing freely in braids down her back and a wide-brimmed black hat sat atop her head.

And the final member of their little group, the one whose eyes were nearly impossible to look away from last night, was wearing another three-piece suit, of course, but this one was a charcoal grey, with a black undershirt, unbuttoned slightly, just enough to show off the top of his sculpted chest. A dark grey tie was loosely tightened around the column of his throat.

And here I was in my ratty old crew neck making my way over to them. What a joke.

"Get their number!" Davia whispered-yelled after me. I rolled my eyes, my face flushing in fear that they might have heard her but as I neared their table none of them reacted at all.

After what seemed like the longest walk in my life, and also entirely no time at all, I was at their table. Four pairs of eyes turned to me, and heat pooled in my core under their intense gazes.

"Um…" Speak, Athena. Come on, say words. You know what words are right? Say them! "Hi."

Death itself could come for me right now and I would welcome it.

Their eyes watched me for a moment before three of their faces split into wide grins. Not the man in the suit, of course not. It didn't look like he knew how to smile, but the others did. And god, if that didn't make me feel like a million bucks.

"Sup?" The tattooed man said in his sinfully chasmic voice, a twinkle in his honey eyes. I couldn't stop the laugh that fell from my lips.

"Oh god, I'm probably just the most articulate girl you've ever met, huh?" Words, nice. I silently thanked my subconscious and my mouth for cooperating. The tattooed man's smile deepened and he let out a small chuckle. The sound was so fathomless that I felt it directly in my core. I watched his throat move with his laugh. A dark tattoo of a snake circled his neck, traveling up the side of his throat. "I, um, sorry. I'm Athena." I waved. Fucking waved. Like a dork. Ok, ground, swallow me up anytime now, please.

"Athena…" The woman replied, her voice was a rich rasp, almost melodic. She said the word as if it was the most delicious thing she's ever had on her tongue. My name had never sounded so delectable.

"I saw you all at the Crabby Crave last night." Fuck, no. "Wait, the Crave Crabbing. Shit. I mean the Craving Crab." Ugh, I need them to stop looking at me like that.

"Yeah, we saw you too." The shorter blonde said with a delectable southern accent that made me feel like I was in an episode of Yellowstone, their eyes meeting mine and holding me there in a comfortable embrace of gazes.

They saw me too. They noticed me.

Good thing you can't hear someone's internal screaming, because AHHHHHHHHHHH!

My head turned to look at the man in the suit. He hadn't said a word since I arrived, his arms cautiously crossed in front of him as if he were bored with the entire encounter. I cleared my throat, ok enough being turned on. Time to get answers.

"I'm sorry if this is awkward, but um-" Ok, time to be honest, no matter how embarrassed I felt. "I was wondering if you saw anything last night because I think the guy I was with drugged me and I wanted to see if you saw where we went. Or what happened…" The words tumbled out of my mouth. It sounded pathetic. But also, anger coursed through my veins at the fucking thought that I needed to be worried about this at all. Stupid Louis. If he knew what was good for him, he would leave this town and never show his face again. I hated that I was in this position again. But most of all I hated that one single night was threatening to topple the years and years of hard work I put in learning to heal after the last time. Funny how trauma works like that.

The tattooed man nearly growled, an animalistic, threatening sound.

"Sorry, that was incredibly personal. I shouldn't have said anything... I'm sorry." I began to back away, shame blooming in my chest.

"Wait." The tattooed man reached out, his cold hand wrapping delicately around my wrist. A shockwave zipped through me at the contact and I swear to god, I think I whimpered. It seemed I wasn't the only one affected, because he quickly dropped his hand, turned his gaze from me, and cleared his throat.

"Um, please have a seat," the blonde said in that delightful soft southern drawl as they looked at their companion questioningly. Every fiber of my being told me to turn on my heel and walk the other way, that the answers they had for me weren't going to be worth the trouble, but something deeper begged me to stay. I had to know. I slipped into an open chair.

"My name is Laz," the blonde said, smiling warmly at me. Their features were soft and welcoming, but there was an inherent danger to them. Like they might be too perfect, like a porcelain doll. But I wasn't naive enough to think that they could be easily broken. "This is Silas," they continued, pointing across the table to the tattooed man who was still avoiding my eyes.

I nodded my acknowledgment and turned back to Laz.

"I'm Samara," the woman spoke, leaning forward until her head rested on her palms. She was so alluring, so stunning that even her voice felt like it was a siren calling for me, beckoning me out to sea. Her ocean was one I would gladly drown in.

"And the chatty one over there," she pointed with a nod of her head at the man in the suit, "is Orpheus."

It was oddly fitting. In Greek mythology, Orpheus is one of the very few individuals to have traveled to the Underworld and survived, exhibiting power over even Hades himself. Looking at this pale, dark haired man, I could see him taking on the God of the Underworld, and winning.

Orpheus was also incredibly naive and had very little trust in those around him. I guess I'd have to wait and see if he lived up to his name.

"Hello," I said, waving again. What is with me and the waving today? What am I, on Sesame Street?

"So your question," Laz said, slowly bringing my attention from the myth himself. "Yes, we saw something last night." Their eyes darted around the table as if checking in with the others. Oh shit. All awkward tension dissolved from my body and I felt the cold wash of fear blanket me again. No, please. My chest tightened and my breath came in shallow bursts.

"Ok, what did you see? What happened?" I was gripping the edge of my metal seat with such a tight hold that I was worried my fingers might rip through. If it happened again, if I lost another part of myself last night. I don't know if I'm going to be strong enough to hold whatever is left of me together anymore.

Laz took a deep breath, preparing to say something unpleasant. "We saw you two leave together, but you looked…off." Oh no. "We were concerned so we checked your drink." They didn't need to finish their sentence, I knew it was already true, but I guess hearing that my fears were accurate from someone else was validating, and horrifying.

"Ok, so he drugged me and then led me out of the bar…" I needed as much information as these strangers could give me. Even if it broke me.

Laz looked at me as if they thought I might break, which was a fair assessment. I didn't know what my threshold was, but I could tell I was nearing it.

"We followed you out, to make sure that fucker didn't do anything." Silas, the man with the piercings continued. Unlike Laz, his voice was not comforting, or nurturing. No, he was seething. I could feel the anger from here. I felt it too. "When we found you in the alley, he had your dress up around your waist, his pants were down…"

"Fuck," I cried, feeling the hot tears stream down my face. My breathing was ragged and erratic. Flashes played in my mind, replacing Louis' face with his, the monster. I leaned forward, hot tears staining my cheeks, as I felt myself crack. My breathing came in rough spurts. Panic gripping my heart as it did so often.

"No, Athena, don't worry, love." Samara jumped in, reaching a hand across the table toward me, but not quite making contact. "We stopped him before he had the chance."

Relief flooded through me like a tidal wave. The tension dissipated, but not completely. There was still the fear there, of how close I'd gotten to shattering again. God, how could I be so stupid? I looked away from my drink for a minute to read Davia's text, maybe not even that long. I should have known. I shouldn't have gone. I shouldn't have let Davia choose my outfit. I should have learned from the last time. I should have -

"Stop," Orpheus demanded. There was a faint Eastern European lilt to his words.

All eyes at the table turned to him, mine included. I watched him, trying to settle my breathing.

"You don't get to feel one ounce of guilt about what that asshole tried to do to you." It wasn't comforting, it was a command. One I was tempted to follow.

I wiped the tears from my eyes. How had he known I had begun a stupid descent down a victim-blaming spiral?

"Did you take me home?" Laz and Samara exchanged a glance, and Samara nodded.

"Yeah, you were coherent enough to give us your address, and your keys were in your purse. We got you home, and safe. And we stayed only long enough to ensure that you were ok." I nodded mindlessly as I took in this information. These four strangers were my fucking saviors last night. They saved me from a horrific fate, and while the scars from my past were well and truly still in place, they could have been flayed open all over again had it not been for them. Had they not seen me acting differently in the bar, had they not followed me out? If this wasn't a fucking shining example of how being a decent person can save lives, I don't know what was.

"What did you do to him?" I saw the pure rage rolling off of Silas and Laz and Samara certainly didn't look too pleased either. I simultaneously hoped that they didn't hurt him and that they ruined him.

"Sent his sorry ass on his way," Orpheus answered, ever the picture of calm and collected. I was glad that they didn't hurt him, and risked getting in trouble themselves, but a small part of me felt like Louis got off far too easily. "After getting a good hit in." Orpheus didn't smile, but a sort of dangerous smirk graced his thick lips. I watched them closely. Wondering how they tasted.

I couldn't help the nagging thought that Louis didn't go home last night. In a strange area, with no one he knew other than Greg, I don't know where else he might have gone. But I can't say I was too worried about it. He could sleep in the ocean with the sharks for all I care.

Orpheus brought his drink to his lips, covering another smirk as if he knew what I was thinking, and agreed.

"Thank you, all of you, for stopping him." That's all I could say. Words would never be enough. "I wish I could make it up to you somehow."

"You can give us a tour," Silas replied eagerly, his dangerous-looking face turning into a wide goofy smile.

"A tour?" I replied at the same time as Laz. Silas nodded.

"Yeah, we're just passing through, but we'd love to get to know…" he hesitated. "The surroundings," he finished. Orpheus was giving Silas what can only be described as a death glare, and Laz and Samara looked on the fence about the whole ordeal as well. Part of me knew they were probably just taking pity on me, the poor girl who got drugged last night. But another part of me could not pass up the chance to spend a few more hours in their intoxicating presence.

"Of course." Silas' eyes lit up at that. "It's the least I could do." Suddenly, I was making plans to meet these four beautiful strangers at the pier in one hour, and exchanging phone numbers with Silas to 'keep in touch'. I didn't miss the way Laz's eyes flashed, or Samara grumbled when Silas insisted that I only needed his number and he could act as a liaison.

I must have looked like a damn zombie when I arrived back at Davia's table after the four of them had left the diner because she was out of her seat pulling me into her arms.

"What did they say, I saw you crying. Oh god, what did they see?" Davia was a good friend. The best friend. But a huge part of me didn't want to burden her with this. Plus, she was so happy with Greg, and I know that if she knew about what his friend did, she would dump his ass flat. She knew what happened to me back then, in fact, she was one of the few who took my side without question. She was intimately aware of why something like this would break me. I didn't want to weigh her down with my issues. Again.

"They just said that Louis walked me out, and they saw us go our separate ways." Davia's relief was palpable. I hated that I had lied to her, but like it or not, there is a stigma in this world for victims of this kind of crime. Something I learned the hard way. This is my home, I don't want rumors and accusations to start flying in my direction again, not when The Maine Plotline is in such a delicate spot financially already.

I knew the truth, and that's really all that mattered to me. Nobody else needs to know.

After finishing breakfast, I excused myself to go change for my tour, a thrilling shiver of anticipation traveling up my spine the whole way home.

SAMARA

SIX

"You're a fucking idiot, Silas." Orpheus was once again berating him for suggesting this impromptu 'tour' with Athena. Hmm. Athena. Such a sensual name for such an appetizing woman. Her long red hair was tousled this morning, loose from the confines of its ponytail last night, and my fingers truly itched to be tangled up in it, pulling her closer to me as her mouth feasted on me. That only lasted a moment before I felt ashamed for thinking such a thing.

"You said we have the day, so I want to take the day." Silas' response was logical of course, except for the fact that it was daylight out, and without layers and an umbrella we'd be seriously uncomfortable on this stupid walking tour of Shockgrove, Maine. Silas held a bouquet of pink roses in his grip. I had rolled my eyes when he insisted that we stop at the market to grab them. But I did have to agree that the flower reminded me of Athena. Pink, like the blush on her face last night at the bar when we walked in, but prickly and strong when in the face of danger. She would like them.

"You wanted to see that she was fine, she was fine." Orpheus ran his hands

"You saw her, Orpheus. She is anything but fine." He was right. She looked like she might fall apart at the seams at any given moment, it was a true challenge to keep my hands to myself, and not reach for her.

"I agree with Silas," Laz spoke from their spot under the awning. We had sprinted over to the pier where we were to meet Athena and sought shelter from the blistering sun under a blue and white striped awning to a closed ring toss game. Too bad, I would have been so good at this game.

"Of course you do, you were head over heels last night." Orpheus threw his hands up in defeat, turning to lean against one of the metal support beams.

Last night, Athena had been in bad shape. Her blood was fucking toxic, it didn't even smell good, so you know that means it had some serious shit in it. Her heart was beating over time to try and keep her alive, keep her safe. Louis almost killed her, just to get laid. If Orpheus hadn't already ripped his head off and tossed him in the ocean, I might have torn off his dick and gagged him with it. There was nothing I hated more than a man who took advantage of women. Even with my tight grip on my control, it was fucking difficult to maintain my relatively calm demeanor after seeing the position she was in.

"Is her blood clean today?" Silas turned to ask Laz. They shook their head.

"Samara got as much as she could out, and it's definitely lessened, but the scent is still there." Laz was angry, their forehead creased with worry.

"I couldn't smell her, not really." Silas slumped down onto the ground, with his back against the booth.

"And why the hell are you trying to smell her?" Orpheus threatened.

Silas turned his eyes to the ground and shook his head as if he was trying to find the words. We all watched him expectantly.

"Oh fuck no," Orpheus exclaimed, having discerned something from Silas' silence and his emotion that I had not yet garnered.

"What?" Laz asked, eagerly.

"You've got to be fucking kidding me." I'd never seen Orpheus so annoyed, and insistent. And that is saying something.

"What the hell is going on?" I chimed in, their head turned to where I stood and I offered a glance that told them not to test me.

"Silas here thinks Athena is his mate," Orpheus fumed as if he was uttering the most outlandish phrase in the entire universe. As if there was a zero in a million chance of it being true.

I was obliged to agree with him.

Although

"How dare you?" Laz dropped to their knees before Silas, their hands finding the collar of his shirt.

"Hey, watch it! You'll stretch the fabric." Silas pushed Laz back, but they didn't drop their hands.

"Fuck your fabric!" They seethed.

"What is your fucking problem?" Silas stood, retreating from Laz's grasp, setting his roses down on the ground, safe from Laz's assault. I turned to Orpheus who was studying Laz intently.

"Abso-fucking-lutely not!" Orpheus looked like he was about to throw both Laz and Silas off the pier. "Not you too." His gaze burned into the side of Laz's face. I turned to them. They were fiery, and growling, all the things they normally are not.

Thinking back to last night, I could sense Laz's reluctance to leave her alone, but that couldn't have been because of any mate bond. They were just worried about her. Like I was. And she certainly isn't my mate.

Silas understood what Orpheus was getting at and when his gaze retrained on Laz, I saw the whites of his eyes darken with a red hue. Fuck. "She's mine," he hissed.

I looked over at Orpheus for a sign of what we should do, and I saw that he was already on his way to restrain Silas. I stepped up behind Laz and placed my hands on their shoulders, firm, but not to the point of pain.

"We are in public, during the day. Both of you cool the fuck off." Orpheus was our leader for two reasons, he was at one point the only person any of us could trust in the entire world, and he had this uncanny ability to put all of us in our place without even really trying.

But right now, it wasn't working.

"You do not get to claim her." Silas was screaming, if there was anyone else on this pier they would hear him no problem. This was dangerous.

"Neither do you," Laz replied, their tone a much more sinister drawl. Quieter, but in no capacity was it any less threatening.

"Hey, look at me," I called out, loud and firm. Laz turned their head slightly to put me in their periphery, never taking their eyes off their current opponent. Silas' eyes darted from me to Laz and back rapidly.

"Athena is not your mate." They both simultaneously hissed at the mention of her name. "She was bleeding last night, and neither of you felt the bond snap in place. Did you?" I know it hadn't because if it had, they would not have been able to control their frenzy until their cocks were in her and her blood was in them. The mating bond was not a subtle thing. It was powerful, raw, and animalistic. They would know if she was their mate. Plain and simple. None of this, 'I think' crap.

"No." Laz was the first to answer, their shoulders relaxing slightly under my palms. I trained my gaze on Silas, prompting him to answer. His calm took a few more seconds to wash over him, the whites of his eyes returning as the red retreated.

"No," he responded eventually, his breathing settled back to its normal rhythm.

"Then there's your answer. She's not your mate. So calm the hell down and stop acting like fresh turns." It was a bit of a vampiric slur for a newly turned creature. Usually synonymous with those who could not control themselves or their impulses. Exactly what these two fools were doing now.

They settled down, the tension dissipating. I sighed. I loved my coven. They were like a family to me. No, not just *like* a family, they were my family.

The only one that mattered at least. One hundred and seventy-three years ago I had a mother and a father, but they did not have a child. They had a bargaining chip. They had a toy whose company they would sell to the highest bidder. My family saw an opportunity in my sharp features and thick curves. They saw the chance to get out of their current predicament, to escape. My flesh was their key to a new life.

And theirs was the key to mine.

Orpheus found me one night, hiding outside the brothel where my family had sent me to entertain for the evening. His harsh words and dominant personality scared me at first. He asked what I was doing, and I don't know why, but I told him everything, every little detail about my pathetic existence. It felt almost euphoric to tell someone else. To let them in on my secrets.

When I was finished, Orpheus got very quiet, his face stoic in an unreadable expression. Then he reached into his purse and grabbed a few coins. Exactly the price I had just finished telling him that my parents often charged for my company. My heart sank, and the euphoria I felt, feeling not so alone even just for a moment, drifted away as I nodded, wiping away the tears. Then I sank to my knees before him. He only wanted what everyone else wanted.

Or so I thought.

He pulled me up to my feet and growled. Yes, actually growled at me. And then he said the words that I have never forgotten no matter how many moons I've lived to see on this Earth. "You will never have to give any more of yourself than you are willing to give, ever again."

For one month, my parents would set "appointments" for me at the brothel. When I would go, I'd find Orpheus had already convinced the gentlemen to leave, and he would pay the price and ask for not a single thing in return. So for one month, I would visit the brothel, have a short conversation with Orpheus, take his money, and leave. I later learned that Orpheus 'convincing' those men consisted of him drinking their blood and hiding their bodies. I didn't know that at the time, he wasn't the bad guy, the men who were paying for a piece of my unwilling flesh were. I can't say I would have been too upset had I known their fate even then.

A large part of me feared that this man's generosity would eventually wear out, that one day he would see how little he gained from our interactions and he would demand payment in kind for the things he's done for me. But even after one month, that day never came.

I'd come to trust him, in a way that I barely even trusted myself. When he offered me the chance at a new life, it was the fastest yes I've ever said. And when he told me the price of my new existence, it was the fastest price I've ever paid.

Silas, Alora, and Laz joined our little coven not long after, each with their own stories of why an eternity as a creature of the night seemed like a better fate than the one they had been sentenced to. I shook off the sharp pain in my chest at the thought of her name.

We were a family, and nothing pained me more than seeing my family at odds with each other. Not in the sense of Silas pushing Orpheus' buttons and riling him up, but something like that… a mating bond…that could ruin the foundation of my little family. And that was something I simply couldn't have.

"There she is," Silas exclaimed, grabbing his roses from the ground, his eyes fixing on a point at the far end of the pier. He was smiling like a love-sick fool. Maybe he should seduce the poor girl, and fuck her to get her out of his system.

But one look at Laz and their smitten expression as they watched her approach, told me that simply couldn't work. No, if we were going to remain a family, nobody could have Athena.

"Behave," I heard Orpheus whisper as the bike approached. She had changed. Her form was now draped in a casual grey t-shirt dress, with a light jacket slung over her shoulders. Her hair had been tamed and loosely curled too. And her face was made up to have that natural 'no-makeup' look. You know the one that all the guys truly believed took no time and effort, but in reality, probably took a good twenty minutes of intense work to get the shading just right. The others won't see the effort she put into this little tour, but I do. And fuck, I like what I see. Her breasts were perky and thick, they bounced slightly as she dismounted her bike. I caught a glimpse of black lace panties as her dress rode up, and suddenly my clit was throbbing. Begging for the chance to rub against those panties and what lies beneath them.

I turned to look at the others, and of course, Laz and Silas were nearly drooling, their eyes were one second from falling out of their sockets. Orpheus was the picture of unphased, but I noticed the way his jaw tensed and his fists balled. He liked what he saw too.

Damn, this girl has some serious magic or something. Why the hell were we all reacting this way for some human?

The word echoed around my head. 'Mate'. That wasn't possible, was it? Not for them, and certainly not for me.

She approached cautiously, timidly. I found myself stepping forward to greet her so that Silas and Laz could get a metaphorical grip on their cocks and calm the fuck down.

"Hi," she spoke, her stunning green eyes bearing into mine.

"Hi, Athena," I responded, once again loving the way her name felt on my tongue. I bet more about her would feel great on my tongue too.

"So, what brings you to Shockgrove?" She steered the bike to a post and locked it up before smiling back at me, her eyes giving me her full attention. I loved it.

"Just passing through on the way to our destination," Orpheus answered before anyone else could. A strange expression crossed her face as she absorbed that.

"Yep, just a couple of Wanderers," Silas teased, knowingly. I thought Orpheus was going to strangle him.

"Well, unfortunately, this isn't Shockgrove's most…exciting time of year." She sighed. Silas held out the bouquet of roses and her sweet eyes landed on them, widening in shock.

"Oh, wow these are gorgeous. Thank you." She smiled, bringing the roses to her nose and inhaling.

"They're from all of us," Laz interjected, and I shot Silas a look that told him not to fight back right now.

"Well, then thank you all." She made sure to make eye contact with each of us as she said those words. Then she turned and headed down the pier. I sent a glance to the others who made quick work of donning their long sleeve jackets, sunglasses, and hats. It wasn't a particularly sunny day, with the clouds blanketing the sky in a soft embrace, but I knew as well as the others did that the rays could still do their damage. I pushed open my black, Victorian-era parasol and followed after Athena, struggling to keep my eyes from her round ass as she walked.

Maybe we could all have a little fun together before we left? Hell, why was I thinking of that? We'd never done something like that together. I had never been attracted to my companions, partly because they are too important to me and sex can ruin even the strongest of relationships, and two, because I wasn't the least turned on by the idea of dick. The feel, the look of them, and the people they were generally attached to. I was very happy finding my pleasure in the sweet folds of women.

So why is it that this gorgeous woman with blood-red hair and pale skin has me thinking of sharing her with my friends?

It would be simple, I would bury my face in her sweet heat, tasting every inch of her release with my tongue while Laz took her nipples into their mouth and Silas fed her his tattooed cock. She would squirm under our hold, straining to get away from the sheer blinding pleasure I was wringing from her body, only to spear herself on Silas' dick. The act of sucking cock never appealed to me, but right now I couldn't stop picturing what her thick lips would look like stretched to accommodate my well-endowed friend.

"I can smell your arousal from here," I heard Orpheus whisper in my ear.

He was a few steps behind me, but my hearing was impeccable. "Please don't tell me that you are going feral over this human too?" His voice was strained. Worried. He knew as well as I did that a mating bond would ruin the delicate family dynamic we've created and protected over the years.

"She's attractive. That's all." I believed the words, but my heart seemed to throb at the idea of her being nothing to me.

Strange.

"We cannot get distracted." Orpheus had taken a few strides to fall into step with me. Silas and Laz had flanked Athena and were asking her questions fitting for a tourist. 'How long does the season last?' 'What events does the city hold?' 'What is the best seafood place?' 'Does this town have a sex shop?'

My head snapped toward Silas whose honey eyes had darkened with sexual promise as he asked her that last question. Her face flushed a deep crimson. The blood beneath her skin burned hot with embarrassment.

Orpheus groaned and rolled his eyes.

But Laz, Silas, and I awaited her response eagerly.

"Yes, we do have one. I can show you…if you'd like." She looked up at Silas through the dark frame of her eyelashes, batting them twice before shyly looking away, her fingers toying with the pink roses in her arms. Ohh, she was good.

"Fuck yeah." Silas nearly jumped up and down at the idea of visiting a sex shop with Athena. The idea did sound kind of appealing.

"What was that you said about getting distracted?" I teased Orpheus, who had crossed his arms and was staring daggers at the back of Silas' head.

"Don't act like you aren't aware of what is coming after us, Samara. You understand more than any of us the danger we're in."

Nameless.

The violent, horrific group of hunters called themselves Nameless because they knew that if our kind ever were to find their identities behind their stupid masks, we would devour them like the weak, pathetic cowards they are.

The faceless legion had been around for centuries, passing their wicked legacy from generation to generation.

These Hunters were cruel, vicious monsters who not only aimed to eradicate all vampires from existence but to make us suffer violent deaths. Deaths that lasted for weeks, months even, draining us of our energy, and powers. Methodically torturing us within an inch of expiration until we had no choice but to beg for a swift death that Nameless would lord over us until the moment that all fight had left and we were nothing but an empty husk that once was full of life.

I was one of the few who escaped their clutches. But my wife was not so lucky.

I shuddered at the memory of the lost fifth member of our coven.

"I know, Orpheus." He was right. We had escaped - albeit not all of us - but Nameless has our essence, they have our scent and they do not take lightly to their captives escaping. In fact, in all the years they've operated as a threatening shadow chasing our kind at every turn, no one else has ever escaped their clutches the way our coven had.

All except for Alora.

But she was the reason we survived, she was the reason we escaped. Her flesh was the key to our new life...

"We can't stay here, they'll find us." They would always find us. My unspoken response hung in the air between us. We knew it was true.

"We can't run forever, what good is a life unlived?" The others sometimes said my optimism was useless and unfounded, but my wife gave up her life so I could be here today. I wasn't going to waste a second of it.

"I don't like the way they look at her," I turned to see his face, his dark brows furrowed, a slight crease forming on his forehead.

"What are you getting from them?" I asked, knowing that Orpheus had been using his ability on the two of them by his concentrated stare.

He inhaled deeply, his eyes fluttering closed for only a second before he sighed. "They're smitten like a bunch of teenagers." I didn't need Orpheus' ability to read emotions to gather that. Laz was laughing at every word Athena was saying as if she was the most humorous person alive, and Silas was taking every chance he could to lean in and whisper in her ear, which always earned him a deep red blush.

"And you aren't much better," Orpheus remarked, turning his annoyed glare to me. I rolled my eyes.

"I'm not smitten," I scoffed. "I simply think she'd be a great lay." Orpheus ran his hands through his perfectly combed hair, messing it up to the point that he looked less put together, and more rugged. He was a handsome man if you liked that sort of thing, but he was truly his most breathtaking when he was about to fly off the handle.

"You're supposed to be the sane one," he nearly growled.

"Do you think there's any merit to their claim?" I asked him, letting my eyes drift back to the display of juvenile courtship happening in front of us.

Athena was telling a story about the origin of the amusement park at the end of the pier. The Ferris wheel and single roller coaster stood tall against the backdrop of the cloudy sky. Hundreds of booths and carts littered the space at their base. But here it was, a warm nearly summer day, and the gates were locked tight.

How these businesses survived this town during the off-season was perplexing.

"About her being their mate?" I nodded. "Absolutely not." Vampires mating with humans was not uncommon. In fact, it was pretty frequent. But the improbable part was the two vampire mates. Multiple mates were rare, accounts of them only really occurred in royal families or for the most powerful of our kind.

"You sound incredibly sure," I mused. I mean, I was sure too. I think.

"You said yourself, she was bleeding last night and the bond didn't snap into place. They would have known the second they scented her blood." I nodded, that was my reasoning too, but a nagging thought kept prickling at the edge of my mind.

Her blood felt strange last night. It was full of that toxic shit the blonde man had slipped her, it wasn't even appetizing, and that is definitely saying something considering before last night I hadn't fed in almost two weeks. So maybe the bond didn't snap because her blood wasn't her own last night? There was something strange about the way we all reacted to her being threatened. Even Orpheus had lost his cool, breaking his own rule to not kill the boy.

"Right." We came to a stop in front of a plain brick building off the beaten path. The outside was unassuming, specifically designed to camouflage the debauchery within.

There was a single neon sign in the window that told us they were open. Athena looked bashful, looking down at her feet.

"Here you go," she said to Silas, who was smiling at her like she was his next meal. He walked toward the door but turned back to look at her.

"You coming in?" She blushed, and I felt my core tighten at the look of her blood rushing beneath her perfect skin. I glanced at Orpheus, ready to take his verbal abuse at my reaction, but he was too busy staring at her face. His expression was empty, but there was a sort of heat behind his gaze.

Athena followed Silas into the shop, and Laz was close behind. Orpheus finally looked at me once she was out of view.

"So, this is getting complicated." He groaned and found a spot against the outside wall to lean. It was clear he wasn't going to go inside. And I almost didn't either, but there was a strange draw, like an invisible string begging me to follow after her. I obliged.

The store was like many others of its kind I've seen in my years. Dark red and purple walls and lushly decorated shelves. Phallic and damn near painful-looking contraptions lined the walls. A back wall was covered entirely in various lingerie, I tried not to picture Athena in the red nightie that would match her flaming hair perfectly.

Silas and Laz were arguing off in the corner, my advanced hearing picked up only parts of their frustrating pissing match. 'She's mine,' 'She looked at me first.'

and on and on. I tuned them out and walked over to where Athena was quietly pursuing the aisles.

"I'm sorry that Silas convinced you to bring us here, he can be…childish sometimes," I said as I approached her. She smiled sweetly, a slight dimple deepening on her cheek. I watched it with rapt fascination.

"It's ok, I don't mind. I actually come here often." Her eyes widened as she realized what she just admitted to me. "Um, not like 'often' but sometimes. I've been here. Once, or twice. At least once. Oh god, I should shut up now," she spoke quickly with an anxious burst. I smiled and watched her face deepen with another blush.

"You don't need to feel embarrassed for taking your sexual pleasure seriously," I whispered. Her gaze locked on mine and I eyed the spot on her neck where her vein was pulsing loudly, tauntingly. "Do you have a favorite?" I asked boldly, waving a hand toward the various toys on display. She coughed to hide her shocked gasp.

"Um, I'm sorry?" She nearly spat out.

"Don't be sorry, give me a good recommendation," I flirted, which felt wrong, but also entirely right.

"Oh, um well that depends on what kind of.." she lowered her voice, I glanced over her shoulder at Laz and Silas who were still engrossed in their own conversation. "Stimulation you prefer?"

I smirked at her, my tongue darting out to wet my bottom lip, she tracked the movement.

"Well, I'm very gay, if that's what you're asking." She gulped, awkwardly and I chuckled. "But I enjoy a good penetration when it's the right person performing it."

She nodded, the scent of her arousal making my mouth water.

"You might like one of these then," she offered, avoiding eye contact now, studying the roses in her hand.

"What about you, Athena? What kind of stimulation are you a fan of?" It was pretty clear based on her reaction to Silas that she liked men, and if the way her breath was coming in shallowly, I could venture a guess that she was just as attracted to me as I was to her at this moment. Call me selfish, but I wanted to hear her say it.

"I'm bisexual," she whispered and a sweet smile spread across her lips. I wanted to taste it.

"Lucky me," I said the words before I could even stop myself, her chest was heaving and I felt like I was going to implode any moment.

"I don't normally talk about it so openly," she admitted shyly, but her eyes never left mine.

"Why not?" I asked.

She swallowed deeply, her eyes flicking to my lips and back.

"I've had.. I've got some stuff I've been working through. It's taken a long time to be comfortable with it again." I noticed how her heart rate picked up, coupled with the far-off look in her eyes.

"Hardships make us stronger. I know I am who I am today because of all the shit I had to go through. I'd wager you are too" Athena's eyes held a deep empathy that I remembered seeing in Orpheus' eyes that first day we met. I reached a hand to her, unable to resist, and ran my fingers delicately against her cheek.

The moment I touched her skin, I felt a shock wrack through my body, like a lightning bolt. I pulled back instantly, picturing Alora's disappointed face in my mind.

"Sorry, I shouldn't have done that," I rushed out before turning on my heel and hightailing it out of the shop. It took most of my focus to not run at full speed, but the cool Maine air hitting my face was a calming sensation. I took a few steadying breaths.

"You shouldn't have gone in," Orpheus spoke from his casual position against the wall. I turned around, finding his eyeing me carefully.

"I know." I walked over, found a space on the wall next to him, and got comfortable.

"Your emotions are all over the place," he confirmed what I already knew. "What's wrong? Don't tell me you think she's your mate too?" He begged. I chuckled half-heartedly, although it didn't really seem all that humorous.

"No, I don't think she's my mate." I let my head hit the wall behind me, taking a deep breath. "I already had one." Alora wasn't my mate in that mystical, fate-filled way, but she was my everything. She was my lifeline. My heartbeat. It had been years since she was taken from me, but even the vivid rush of desire I was feeling in my core had me feeling sick to my stomach with guilt.

I wouldn't want someone else. I promised Alora she'd be my one and only. I swore it to her before our friends and the stars of fate. Just because she's gone, doesn't mean that vow is any less iron-clad now than it was that day.

"Samara," Orpheus started. I let my head fall so I could look in his direction. "Alora would want you to feel love again, she would never want to keep you from experiencing the happiness that she used to bring you again." I smiled lightly at the memory of her bright blue eyes. "Just don't go trying to find it with this human, ok? Please?" He was exasperated, an emotion I didn't often see in him.

I laughed, fully and leaned my head on his broad shoulder. "I promise." I meant it, but I hoped I could keep it.

A few minutes later, Athena exited the shop followed by Laz and Silas, who was now holding a shopping bag. He had a mischievous glint in his eyes and I suppressed the urge to roll mine.

Athena resumed her tour, leading us down to the pier again, spending quite a bit of time on each of the shops along the way. She spoke so highly of the businesses on the boardwalk and their owners, it was admirable how much she respected them.

After a while, we came to a stop outside a small storefront just down the pier from the amusement park. Its worn red awning was weathered and tattered but in a cute vintage way. The windows were filled with shelves of books and cute wooden tables and cozy padded chairs. Gold Painted lettering graced the window, 'The Maine Plotline'. Cute.

"This is my store." My head snapped to Athena, she looked shy, as if she was embarrassed about her accomplishment of owning a store.

"You own this place?" I asked, realizing it was the first I'd said to her since we left the sex shop. She smiled and nodded.

"I do." She tossed a forlorn glance over her shoulder at the quaint storefront.

"Can we go inside?" I don't know why I felt the need, but I wanted to see if her business had the same kind of quaint charm that her home had. To see if her essence was plastered on every wall as it had been in her cottage. I smiled as I thought of her charming abode, and how perfectly it reflected this shy, bubbly woman in front of us.

"Oh, yeah sure." She fumbled through the pocket of her jacket for her keys and made quick work of the lock before stepping aside to allow us inside. "Please come in. I'm going to put these in water."

As we followed her into the shop, I noticed once again how intoxicating her scent was. I still couldn't smell her blood, but she had this almost wintergreen scent to her and it reminded me of a cozy winter day.

The first thing I noticed as we arrived in the shop was the colors. She had painted the walls with an almost ivy green, deep, thought-provoking, sensual. The light brown shelves sat against the walls, filled from floor to ceiling with books. Old titles, with worn and tattered covers, all the way to new arrivals, the scent of the printed words still prevalent. There was a small counter where there was a coffee machine and some pastries behind a glass case.

Sections of the store had been blocked off for small group and individual reading areas. Lush green velvet couches and plush black armchairs created an almost private feel.

It was gorgeous. Personal. Intimate. Everything I'm learning to expect from Athena.

"This place is incredible," Laz said, their fingers trailing over the spines of some books.

"Thank you," Athena responded, returning with a glass vase and placing the roses on the counter, a bright smile spreading across her face. Her features were soft and kind. Almost innocent. But her eyes held a sort of darkness that I found entirely too familiar.

"Have you had it long?" Silas asked, moving closer to her. He hadn't touched her again since this morning at breakfast, but that wasn't stopping him from getting as close as possible. A rush of jealousy spiked in my chest.

What the hell? Jealous?

A harsh sadness crashed over me at the thought of my late wife again. It's been years since we escaped Nameless, years since Alora sacrificed herself for our freedom. I've found myself attracted to other women since then, I've even indulged in some heavy petting, but I had not yet crossed the line and slept with one. I always stopped myself before it got that far. I couldn't stand the thought of her not being the last woman I was with. Alora wasn't my mate, but that didn't make our love any less powerful and genuine. The loss of her was potent and painful. Less and less each day, but still raw enough to sometimes take my breath away. I hated that I was feeling this way over someone new, having these dark thoughts, these dirty fantasies of Athena when it should be my wife that I'm thinking of.

How does one ever move on from a grief so potent? How can someone ever breathe again? How can you not hate yourself for developing feelings for someone else?

I took a deep breath and crossed the space until I was far enough from Athena to take a breath without inhaling her wintergreen scent.

The sooner we left Shockgrove, the better.

SILAS

SEVEN

Her body was a magnet. A powerful force drawing me into her orbit, holding me in place, and keeping me hostage in her universe. The moment my hand touched her skin at that dingy diner, the world around me ceased to exist. I had never felt so completely and totally absorbed by a person the way her energy consumed me.

She has to be my mate.

I feel it.

Orpheus and Samara were right, logically I knew that. She was bleeding last night, and although I had gone a little feral when beating that sorry excuse for a man, no bond had snapped into place.

I've been protective my whole life, hell, I'd kill for any one of The Wanderers and I have. But to feel so defensive of this human so quickly, to know that without a doubt I'd lay down my life at her feet if it meant her safety…that had to mean more.

I listened to her, excitedly telling the tale of the amusement park on the pier, and I hung on to every word as if it was the most interesting thing I'd ever heard. And from her lips, it was. I wanted to taste her, to sink to my knees and run my tongue over her center, send her into a shattering orgasm where she could do nothing but scream my name. I wanted to wear her thighs around my head like a crown. I wanted her. Plain and simple.

Laz was walking on thin ice, I don't know who they thought they were, laying a claim on her, when it was so evident that she was mine. I shook my head, allowing the murderous thoughts toward my companion to drift away. Athena seemed to enjoy their company, they made her laugh. And fuck, that laugh was one of the most glorious sounds in the world, so if Laz was the reason for it, I'd allow them to be near her. For now.

Athena led us through her bookstore and I found myself mapping out all the surfaces I'd like to claim her on. The counter, the velvet couches, up against the bookshelves, having her pant and moan as pages fell from the sky from the impact of my cock in her soft folds.

Orpheus and Samara had taken to looking at one of the shelves near the front of the store; she'd been wearing a strange expression ever since she ran out of the sex shop. Laz followed Athena as she led them deeper into the store's depths. I watched as Athena smiled, describing the changes she's made to the decor in the last few years. I didn't care much about decor, or feng sway, or whatever she called it. All I knew is that this store was important to her, and therefore it was important to me.

"So, you're a bit of a bookworm then are you?" I teased, wetting my lower lip with my tongue and loving the way her green eyes traced the movement.

"I've been reading since before I can remember," she responded, her skin flushing again. I fucking loved making her blush.

"What kind of books do you read?" I took a step toward her, boxing out Laz who seethed behind me. They can suck my dick, it was my turn to have her attention.

I towered over her by at least a foot, and I loved that difference. She had to look up at me as I came closer, her neck straining under the movement. I watched the vein beneath her skin throb and I felt my fangs elongate slightly in anticipation. "I'm a fan of fantasy." She managed to say, but the breathless way her words came out told me she was as affected by our proximity as much I was.

I circled her, coming to stop behind her. I brought my lips close to her ear and whispered. "I'm a fan of romance. But none of that PG shit. No, I like the down-and-dirty stuff." I saw her swallow, the movement making her pulse quicken. I wanted to taste her blood so desperately. I was thankful I was behind her, so she couldn't see the way my fangs begged for her. I saw Laz staring at us, a sort of hungry jealousy in their eyes.

"Yeah, smut is pretty good," she responded in a near whisper. I watched her chest heave and the scent of her arousal nearly had me shifting right then and there.

I kept my face near her neck, letting my breath paint her skin with beautiful bumps, as my hands trailed the books on the shelf next to me. I didn't know these titles, but I was willing to bet something called "Devour Me" was going to be exactly what I needed. Careful not to touch her again, I reached around her until I was holding the book open in front of her face, my lips so close to her ear I could feel the pulsing of her blood in my fangs. I flipped the pages as her breathing became labored.

"Hmmm, let's see here." I stopped on a delicious-looking page and began to read. "'Her skin was slick with sweat as Drake hovered over her. His tongue traced a roadmap across her exposed skin, teasing her sweet flesh before taking one of the mounted peaks of her breasts into his mouth.'" I felt her tense beneath me, not in fear, but in pure anticipation. Laz was watching her with ravenous intentions. As long as they keep their hands to themselves, they can watch. I liked putting on a show. "'She felt his hands travel down her sides until his fingers dug into her thighs as he spread them apart, revealing her hot center, slick with desire for him.' Oh, this is getting good, don't you agree, Athena?" She nodded, wordlessly, her eyes glued to the pages I held open in front of her. I inhaled, prepared to continue, but the sound of her sweet voice stopped me.

"'His fingers trailed the sensitive skin near her core and she moaned. One brush of his touch against her clit was all it took for her to detonate. Her body raged with a flash of blinding heat as Drake slid a finger inside her folds. Stretching her. Pleasing her.'" Her words were breathy and sultry, and I felt my cock spring to life. It took every ounce of willpower I wasn't already diverting to controlling my shift to keep myself from pressing it up against her ass. I flicked my eyes to Laz, the outline of their arousal evident as well.

"Keep going, baby girl," I whispered into her ear and her lips parted to let a moan escape. It was the most captivating sound I'd ever heard. I would give anything to hear it again.

"'His cock was hard against his jeans and she reached for him, begging him to let it spring free and give her the pleasure she was aching for.'" Her scent grew stronger, more intoxicating. I was so transfixed on her, I barely noticed Samara and Orpheus looming in the stacks behind Laz, their eyes just as full of hunger as mine, I'm sure. Laz took a step forward, nearly touching her, but I didn't mind because their closeness simply made Athena's breath catch and a tiny moan escaped her lips.

"'She clawed at his fabric prison until she reached the prize she was after. His thick length stood erect as he looked down at her naked form, writhing and begging for him.'" Laz leaned forward, their lips dangerously close to her extended neck, she almost leaned into them. I saw the words on the page and before I could stop myself I spoke the line aloud.

"'Beg me to fuck you,' Drake demanded.'" Athena's head lulled back as she exhaled, my words finding their target in the center of her core. Laz and I had her caged in, her body was flush against both of ours and I could tell how much she wanted it. I looked at the next line and felt like I was ready to explode just with the anticipation of hearing her sultry voice read it.

"I believe the next line is yours," I barely recognized my voice, it was primal, hungry. All hers.

I turned my head just enough that I could see her lips, and my companions. Their faces were equally as eager to hear her performance as I was.

"'Fuck me,'" She paused. The room was filled with so much tension I was surprised we all hadn't shifted already. I exhaled, long and deep, my breath landing on her skin as she read the last word. "'Please.'"

I closed the book, slowly, my fingers feeling numb with the ache to touch her again, and placed it back on the shelf. Laz was staring at her, their eyes held a slightly reddish tint, nothing she would notice, but I knew they were close to a shift. Hell, we all were. Even Orpheus, who stood with arms crossed, looked like he might try to devour her any second. And Samara, whose self-control could rival even the most ancient vampires, was teetering on the edge of a shift. All for this human.

My human.

We waited in tension-filled silence for a few moments, her body trapped between mine and Laz's. I'd fuck her right here, if she asked me to. And I'd let my friends watch. Just say the words, bookworm, and I'm yours. I wanted to believe that her arousal was for me alone. But from the way her body reacted to Laz's, I knew it wasn't.

"Yeah, those books are great." She said, matter-of-factly, the heat and desire that was so present in her voice previously was gone. Then she stepped out from my orbit, and moved toward the front of the shop.

If I couldn't smell her arousal still, I might have thought it was all an act.

So my girl likes to play games then? Good.

Let's play.

ORPHEUS

EIGHT

Fuck, this human was going to be the death of all of us. And I mean that quite literally. Her little performance in the bookstore was fucking intoxicating. Samara and I could smell her from the front of the shop, and it was as if our feet moved on their own accord. Drifting across the space until our eyes landed on her. Her face flushed, her chest heaving, her nipples peaked and pressing against the grey fabric of her dress.

The four of us watched her like she was our prey and our most prized possession at the same time. If she didn't break the spell she had on us by walking away, we might have all taken her right then and there. Hell, maybe we should have. Then we could have had a taste of this human that perplexes us so that we could get the hell out of this town. Nameless was after us, and they're never far behind. We cannot stay here, we shouldn't even be here now, but this devil of a woman had to go get into trouble.

As she continued to lead us all across this wretched little town, I began formulating a plan.

We had to leave, and soon. Fuck, we should have left last night after our shots. That was the plan. Silas nearly begged for a reprieve from our travels. We had been running non-stop for nearly four hours at that point. At our speed, we made it through the entire state of New Hampshire and most of Vermont.

Vermont was where we had hunkered down for a few weeks. It was safe enough, the town we found had enough people in it that we felt concealed, but not too many that we felt surrounded. But then we saw the symbol.

Two offset triangles, and a wooden stake. That symbol - painted, printed, projected. It has plagued our kind, like a shadow. No, not a shadow. This was far more sinister. More revealing. Like daylight. When we saw the symbol, it meant that we had been discovered, that Nameless was close. We couldn't hide anymore, just like daylight. They were gifted in manipulation, and scare tactics. It worked. Whenever we noticed the symbol, on a flier in the coffee shops we frequented, or painted on a billboard like some kind of taunting graffiti, we packed up and ran. Nameless had either the best or worst trackers in the world. On one hand, they gave us the chance to run, to get away. On the other, they instilled a sort of fear, a dark panic in us that followed us everywhere. So that even when we found respite, we were never truly free from their influence.

And we never would be.

Not until every last Hunter was killed. And I would not rest until this Earth was rid of their vile corruption.

Although they might say the same about me.

Perspective is funny like that. Hearing this tale, the tale of our kind being chased across the world, tortured within an inch of our lives, and hunted from our side might make a person sympathetic to our cause. However, hearing the same tale from the dirty mouth of a Hunter might change someone's mind about us. Might make them fear us. We were something to fear, of course we were. We kill, we drain, we hunt.

But that's where their tale ends. The Hunters. That's all they need to know in order to justify their attempt to eradicate my kind from the planet. The rest of the story doesn't matter to them. It doesn't matter that my coven only hunts monsters. People like that asshole at the bar last night.

In a sense, we are both Hunters. Nameless and us. Life and death isn't so black and white.

I watched my coven, Silas and Laz mostly, fawn over this red headed human. I also saw cracks in the wall Samara had expertly built around her dead heart. Her kind smile melting the cold exterior we had all so carefully crafted over the dark years since we've been running.

I don't trust her. No, I don't think that she intentionally got drugged and nearly raped as some sort of ploy to keep us in town. I don't think she's working with Nameless. That's not the distrust I feel when I look at her.

When I look at her, when my eyes involuntarily scan her body, appreciating her curves, and catch a glimpse of her twinkling green eyes, I don't think she will betray us. I think she will make us weak.

I feel it happening already, as I watch Silas and Laz. Their emotions tickling my senses like a soft embrace, their sickly sweet feelings toward this human. I felt them at the bar and I feel it more here.

A long time ago, I told my coven about my ability to feel emotions, and they saw it as an invasion of privacy. They didn't tell me that of course, but I felt it. They didn't need to tell me a lot of things that I was able to discern. Every member of The Wanderers is gifted, that's why we've been able to stay hidden from Nameless for so long. That's why we've been able to remain safe - if that's what you want to call it- from many threats over the years. But my particular gift, the way I knew when someone was plotting, when someone was anxious, or when someone was hiding something. It's what made me a good leader then and it makes me a good leader now. It's kept us alive.

They know that as well as I do. I try to refrain from reading them if I can. Sometimes I don't have a choice. Like with this human.

Athena's emotions this morning at breakfast nearly consumed me. Her guilt. As if she had any reason to feel guilt over what that fucker attempted last night.

But what was worse, what truly gripped my soul was her fear. Unrelenting, deep, and broken beyond repair. I wasn't planning on speaking to her. Hell, I don't even want to look at her, but fuck, I was practically choking on her dread and I needed her to stop. For my sake if nothing else.

Now though, those feelings were still there, but dormant, a sort of constant cloud covering her. But the emotion that danced around her was happiness and lust. Both are equally as potent, and distracting.

I knew it was a bad idea to do this tour. Silas' little performance in the bookstore was exhibit fucking A. Her lust, her passion, her fucking aching need entered every single one of my senses at once. Drowning me in her desire. If I hadn't already felt that, the scent of her arousal would have alerted me anyway. Before I could stop myself I was watching. Watching the flushed look on her face, the way she pressed her thighs together to chase some relief, the way her eyes scanned the pages of the book and then landed on me as she said those words.

'Fuck me, please.'

No, I didn't trust her one bit.

"Well other than the lighthouse that's about all." I sighed, thankful that our waste of time has come to an end. It was a relatively warmer May day, and the sun was shining, which justified our hats and sunglasses, but made the long sleeve shirts and suit jackets we wore a bit uncomfortable. But I'd rather experience discomfort than the vicious sting of daylight.

I'm about to demand we make our way out of town when Silas opened his stupid fucking mouth.

"Show us the lighthouse?" I groan, I don't mean to, but it slips out and I see my companions eyes turn to me, Laz and Silas with an edge of fury. But it's her eyes that hold me. She watches me, her eyebrows furrowing. Disappointment dancing around her.

"It's ok, I've monopolized so much of your time already," she whispered, tossing her hands in a 'it's not a big deal' kind of way.

I felt their gazes, their anger, it pressed against the edge of my subconscious. I looked to Silas, then to Laz, then to Samara. They were waiting for me. Of course.

"Show us the lighthouse," I demand. It's not kind, not sweet. But that's not who I am, and if my companions thought they might get a different version of me, then they were fucking naive.

"Right this way," Athena says to me. Her green eyes held mine in an almost challenge until the moment she turned.

So we followed, I barely registered the elbow that Silas threw into my abdomen, he knew that it wouldn't hurt me. That wasn't his intention.

"Could you be less of a dick, please?" He asked.

"Could you be less of a love sick puppy?" I toss back, keeping my eyes trained ahead. Watching. Always watching.

"I saw you looking at her." It wasn't an accusation, or a threat.

"And?" I prompted.

"And… I think you know there's something here." He's referring to the 'mate bond' that he feels so strongly is there. I rolled my eyes.

"If you want to get your dick wet, be my guest, but don't be ridiculous with all this mate crap. You know as well as I do, that she's not your mate." I whisper. Luckily for us, Laz is talking Athena's ear off, asking questions about the lighthouse and its histories. Which she answers truthfully, but with a sort of fond sadness circling her. Interesting.

Silas growled, low, threatening, and I felt his hand come up and grip my arm. I turned my head to look at him for the first time. His eyes were dark, and bloodshot, to anyone he just looks like he needs sleep, but I know what that look is. Intimately.

"How can you be hungry? You fed last night." Our kind could survive on what he had last night for weeks, maybe longer if the vampire was strong enough.

"Because of her, I need her." His voice was laced with desperation. Fuck. So much for leaving after this tour.

"We can't stay here," I toss back, but I know from the look in his eyes that there is no fighting this. If he was already hungry, already craving, there wasn't much I could do to stop this.

"And I can't leave. Not until I know." I may be the leader of this coven, I may make choices that the others follow, but when it comes to this - to primal needs - there is nothing more sacred to our kind than a mate bond, and if Silas was reacting to this human like this, I knew that we were not leaving until he was able to confirm or deny the bond.

"Fuck." I said, running my hands down my face. My mind was already shifting the plans I've made.

When we left Vermont, we knew Nameless would expect us to head West, toward the wide expanse of the United States. We covered our tracks as well as we could, left some breadcrumbs heading that direction, then turned to head East.

It was a stupid idea, heading to the dead end that was Maine. Which is why we made it. Nameless thinks that we are smarter than that. With any luck they won't catch on that we didn't go West for a few weeks.

We can stay for a brief time. It would have to be enough.

"I'll text you an address, meet me there after your fucking tour." Silas nodded, and I felt it. He was sorry, guilty. He didn't want to be the reason we didn't stick to the plan, but there was another emotion that floated through my senses, drifting off of him. Happiness. He wanted to stay with her.

I turned on a heel, not bothering to say anything to my coven or the human who seemed to have them wrapped around her little finger.

I had preparations to make, and not a lot of time to make them.

Looks like Shockgrove's population just grew by four.

ATHENA

NINE

I was still reeling from the…reading… in the bookstore. I don't know what came over me, why I, after being caged between Silas' powerful arms and Laz's strong body with the dirty book in front of us, felt the desire to read aloud. To say those words to them. To all of them. I'd read that book before, and I knew what I was going to read, but I did it anyway. Why? Because of the way Silas smirked at me, because of the way Laz's body gravitated toward me, the way Samara's eyes were on me the moment I stepped off the bike, and because of the way Orpheus, who had done whatever he could to avoid me, had come around the corner and stood among the stacks of books and watched me with ravenous eyes. Or maybe because I felt autonomy over my own desire for the first time in a long time. I felt like I deserved to feel what I was feeling without the guilt or the memories haunting me.

That's why I said those words. And, I think I meant them.

Which might be the most surprising of all, considering my close call last night. After the first time that my monster took what he wanted from me, I didn't feel attached to my body for months. And then when I finally felt like I belonged to myself again, I hated it. Hated the way it felt like I was wearing someone else's body around, trying to force it to fit. I would shy away from anyone who looked at me. Hated the way that no matter how sweet someone was, their faces eventually molded into his. I couldn't be attracted to someone without remembering his words in my ear.

"You've wanted this for so long, haven't you? I can tell."

It took years of therapy and hard work to let myself be aroused without seeing him. And longer to let another person touch me the way he did. But I did it. I found strength and courage, and I moved past what he did to me.

And then it almost happened again. That is why I'm so surprised that even after all that, with the fear and the memories that Louis brought back, I'm attracted to these strangers. No strings or ancient memories attached.

My body feels this intense sort of pull toward them. Not to mention they might have saved my life last night. If not my life, at least my sanity. Hot as sin and respectful? Sign me the fuck up.

Ok, I need to calm down. I nearly dropped to my knees in front of all four of them. Even went out and bought a damn dress to wear for them. Who the hell am I? This doesn't happen to me.

They're not attracted to me, they simply feel sorry for me. They saw me go through something traumatic last night and they're throwing me a proverbial bone. A sexy, dirty-talking, kind, did I mention sexy, bone.

Ok, Athena, stop thinking of bones.

"So, do you come to the lighthouse often?" Laz asked, their gaze was trained on me and their face was the picture of interest. I'm not sure I've ever had such genuine, undivided attention before.

I led the group toward the hole in the gate and smiled at Laz. The waves were crashing against the rocky cliff below the lighthouse, and I could feel the wet sting of the ocean and taste the salted air on my tongue as I breathed. It was more potent here than it was on the pier, with no buildings or roller coasters to block the wind rolling in from the horizon.

"I used to." They didn't push, only nodding gently with a quiet understanding. Laz had this sort of pure and innocent nature to them, but the look in their eyes as they pressed their whole body to mine told me they were anything but. I came to a stop in front of the gate and turned to my companions, only to realize that Orpheus had left. I scanned the direction from which we came for him. Did he just fall behind? Silas came into my line of sight.

"He had an appointment," Silas offered. I nodded, wondering why I suddenly felt sad about his absence. He's barely said a word to me. I shouldn't care that he ditched my tour. But I do, and that feels weird.

"Well, welcome to Shockgrove lighthouse." I smiled and pushed the weakest part of the fence, my mind flooding with memories of my mother doing the very same. Her long auburn hair, her freckled face. She was gorgeous, and I loved every moment I had with her.

Sighing, I moved through the fence, only slightly aware of the others following closely behind.

The last time I was here, life looked quite a bit different.

I swallowed the lump in my throat and forced the tears that threatened to fall back. Her hand was frail, her skin pale. Her hair had lost its illustrious shine and had muted to a dull color. Her head was covered in a small knit hat, concealing the small patches of balding spots that she had developed from her brief stint in chemo. It was obvious pretty quickly that she wasn't going to survive her fight against this illness, and she made the decision not to spend what little time she had in a hospital bed, connected to tubes.

She wanted to die as she lived. Free.

I lead the group of strangers toward the entrance to the lighthouse, fighting off the vivid pictures that begged to be replayed. I hadn't thought of that day for a long time, but now I couldn't seem to keep the memories from flowing.

Me, smiling weakly as I pushed her wheelchair toward the edge of the cliff, close enough that we could feel the mist and see the waves dance along the shoreline below. I always wondered what it would feel like to be the waves. To build and grow until you're so full of emotion, or passion that you finally crash, exploding, sending a small piece of yourself in every direction. To have so much power that you make that big of an impact.

"Ok, let's go up," she said, meekly. She was getting weaker with every passing moment. It's a horrible thing. Watching someone you love wither away, seeing the light that used to shine so brightly behind their eyes dim each day until you know that at any moment the light may go out for good, and you'll be cast into darkness. I'd never been afraid of the dark until the moment I knew what her darkness would mean.

"There's no elevator, mom." She scoffed, tossing a hand toward me. The sleeve of her sweater rode up revealing her arm. Has it always been so skinny?

"Get me to the stairs and I'll climb them." She was so determined, her voice so sure that I almost forgot.

"Mom, you can't." I hated saying it, but it was true. She wasn't strong enough. She hadn't been for days. She's only been able to stand for brief periods of time. There was no way she would be able to climb the tower.

"I can, and you're going to help me." She started wheeling herself toward the base of the lighthouse, and I couldn't shake the terror that pulled at my heart.

When she reached the base of the stairs, the spiral staircase that we had climbed together over a dozen times throughout my life. A climbing staircase that led to a whole slew of adventures that we had with each other.

"I don't remember the last time we climbed these," she mused, her head falling back as she took in the sight of the steps.

"Me either," I responded, quietly. I promised myself the moment I heard she was sick that I wouldn't cry in front of her. She needed me to be strong and that's what I would do.

"You know how everyone always says, 'I wish I knew the last time, was the last time?'" I nodded. "Well, now we do. This time, right now. This will be the last time we climb these stairs together and we're going to make it count." A sob lodged itself in my throat, as she tossed off her blanket. Her legs had lost significant muscle mass, and she also had lost weight so her already small frame looked impossibly tiny. She was so weak, I *saw it in the heaving of her chest, the unwanted hitches in her breathing. She was slipping away, and all I could do was watch her go.*

I moved forward, helping her stand, securing my arm around her waist, and navigating her arm to rest on my shoulders.

Together we stood at the base of the stairs, her fragile weight resting carefully on mine, and began to climb.

As I pushed open the door to the lighthouse, I found myself inhaling a sharp breath. It looked the same. I don't know why I expected it to change. Maybe because everything else had changed so drastically since that day.

"Wow, this place is pretty cool," Silas said as he entered the space. I felt heat then, burning me, licking my skin. I shouldn't be here.

"Athena," I heard my name, but I couldn't place it. The room began to spin and my breathing came in punishing spurts. "Hey, hey, look at me." I felt a presence in front of me, blocking my view of the stairs that were haunting me, but their face was unfocused and blurry.

The moment the stairs were out of my sight, I dashed out of the lighthouse and into the open air. I bounded across the field and stopped at the cliff's edge, letting the cold ocean air caress my skin as I breathed. Flashes. Always flashes. Bits and pieces of this memory with my mom, tainted with the residue of his touch on my skin. One trauma into the other. Like a sliding slope, when I was overwhelmed with one, the other wasn't far behind. I pressed my palm to my chest and forced my breath to come. Forced my eyes to remain open, trained on the horizon, and not focused on the glimpses of pictures that were escaping from the deep recesses of my mind.

"Athena, what's wrong?" I could focus again, the world slowly settling around me. Silas was in front of me, and I felt Laz and Samara flanking either side. Silas' honey eyes were full of concern and worry. He held his ground before me and commanded my gaze. His shoulders were moving up and down in clear and deep breaths. Before I knew it, I was mirroring his movements, my own breathing leveling out.

The panic subsided. The images of my frail mother and the monster who dared to impede on my memories of her locked away tightly, for now. I stood a little taller and nodded to Silas. "I'm sorry," I managed.

"Don't be sorry," Laz said, moving closer, but still maintaining some distance between us. I smiled at them. "I take it this place means something to ya?" I nodded again and was thankful that Laz didn't push. I don't know if I would be able to explain what had just happened to me.

A phone rang and I saw Samara pull it from her bag. She grimaced at the name, and her eyes darted back to me as if she wasn't sure she should leave me.

"I'm ok, it was just a panic attack. I promise I'm ok now." Something in her gaze told me she didn't really believe me. "I promise. It happens sometimes. I'm fine." She fought an internal battle for a moment more before striding off to answer the call.

I turned to Silas. "That's one way to end a tour," I joked and I saw his eyes soften. "I think I dropped my bag in there." I curse under my breath. That's the last thing I need, to go back inside after finally regaining my composure.

Laz took a step forward and I felt a sort of cold radiating off of their body. They watched me carefully, like I may break at any moment.

The two of them exchanged a silent look, one that was too quick for me to decipher. "I'll go get your bag," Laz said eventually, taking cautious steps away like they didn't want to leave me alone with Silas.

With a sigh, they turned on their heel and jogged off toward the structure.

When I turned my head back to the man before me, he was watching me, his entire body closer to mine than he had been before. I shivered from the cold rolling off of him, and from his proximity. He was so close to me now, I could see his dark hair falling out from beneath his hat, and a tattoo peeking out from his collar. The scaled design was intricate and dark against his unusually pale skin. I bit my bottom lip between my teeth.

"Do you want to get out of here?" Those words have gotten a bad rep.

Usually spoken with a slurred speech by drunken frat boys to their catch of the night. But right now, coming from the lips of this handsome tattooed, sinful man in front of me as he watched me with caring eyes, they might just be the best words I've ever heard.

"Please." His eyes glistened with something dark and mischievous at the word, a hungry smirk claiming his lips and I felt the blush heat my face.

"Say that again." His dark timber vibrated deep, his tone gravelly and inviting. A challenge. I took a step forward, involuntarily, as if my feet were being pulled to him. He licked his lips, leaving a sheen across their surface, I watched them hungrily. I knew what he would do if I followed through on his request. And I was shocked to realize that I wasn't afraid. I didn't want to shy away from the affection. I didn't feel phantom hands on my arms as Silas held me. All I felt was him, and I wanted him. All I had to say was one little word.

"Please."

His lips crashed into mine, and suddenly I knew what it felt like to be the waves. It took me all of a moment to kiss him back. His hands snaked around my waist and pulled me flush against his rock-solid form and his lips devoured me.

My hands found the back of his head and my fingers tangled with his hair, pressing his face to mine. His tongue pressed against my lips, begging for entry and I opened, willingly, eagerly. Our tongues collided and I whimpered against his mouth as heat pulsated in my core.

I felt his teeth graze my bottom lip and he let out the most delicious moan I've ever heard. I pressed my mouth to his, trying to taste it. To consume the sounds he made.

One of his hands trailed along my side, up to my throat where he gripped. I gasped at the sensation of lost airflow. It wasn't enough to worry me, just enough to enhance everything I was feeling. My entire body was on fire and beneath his palm, I swear my skin sizzled. Heat and cold. Fire and ice. A passionate, blind, inferno.

Driven wild by this strangely vulnerable yet powerful position he held me in, I took his lip into my mouth, ran my tongue against the piercing there, and bit down.

"Fuck," Silas murmured against my mouth, his hand closing in tighter on my throat until small white dots began forming on the edges of my consciousness. I waited for the panic to rise, but it never did. It was delicious, deviant, and everything I never knew I would enjoy. The difference here was that I knew that Silas would stop if I asked. And that felt powerful. Like I had permission to enjoy this.

His fingers loosened their hold on my windpipe, but his palm remained steadfast against my skin. My breath rushed back to me in a gasp that he swallowed down, hungrily.

I lifted onto my tiptoes, to press into his body as much as I could manage. I clawed at his shoulders, needing more. My clit throbbed with the need to be ravaged by this man. He growled against my mouth, a strained, sinful sort of sound, as his lips pressed against mine.

I was lost in glorious desire, he could have asked for anything in that moment and I would have gladly given it to him. Freely and with my complete consent. I nearly forgot we were on the cliff's edge overlooking the ocean until the crashing of a wave against the cliffs below mirrored the intense beating of my heart.

Our lips separated, but his forehead rested on mine as we both swallowed gasps of air, greedily. My lips felt puffy, satisfied, and frozen, a feeling quite like the moments after finishing an ice cream cone. My lips curled up in a sated smile, and I felt Silas' body shake with incredulous laughter. Finally, we stepped away, he unwrapped his chilled arms from my body and the slightly chilled May air warmed me instantly.

His honeyed eyes were glistening as he smiled brightly at me. He was looking at me as if he had just won a prize, or like he was in awe. He was positively gorgeous and my heart pounded at the thought of him looking at me like that forever.

"You taste incredible, Athena," he remarked, a devious glint in his gaze as he ran his tongue along his bottom lip. I burned. My eyes were locked on his lips, wondering how soon I'd be able to feel them again, wondering how good they'd feel on other parts of my body.

Silas' gaze heated and he took a step forward, I readied myself for another passionate onslaught, but unluckily, or luckily, a voice pulled me from his spell.

"Here's your bag." Laz held my bag up for me, their voice holding a dejected tone, and their gaze avoiding mine. I grabbed it quickly, ignoring the strange feeling of guilt that was bubbling under the surface.

"Thank you, Laz." I tried to meet their eyes, but they kept them trained away from me, their lips pressed in a tight line. They had seen the kiss, of course, they did. We weren't exactly hiding it. Maybe their flirtatious banter wasn't just banter, maybe it wasn't just out of pity.

Maybe they actually liked me? The memory of their hard body against mine at the store came to mind. Would I have kissed Laz if it had been Silas who went for my bag? Yeah, I think I would have. Hell, I would have kissed Samara if she was in their place too.

The thought sent warm tendrils of excitement to my core and a flutter to my heart. How is it that I went from being the town's social pariah with a traumatic past to the town's social pariah with a traumatic past and three incredibly sexy individuals interested in me? Well, maybe not three. Samara ran out of that sex shop pretty quickly and hadn't said more than a few words to me since, but there was a heat in her eyes that I craved to see again.

Someone pinch me.

"We should head out, Silas. Orpheus called." I heard Silas sigh deeply before walking toward them. "Thanks for the tour, Athena." Laz tossed, stopping Silas in his tracks and moving away rapidly. Silas paused, watching after his friend, and I suddenly felt like a horrible person. All euphoria that had invaded my senses from our kiss was evaporating with each languid step Laz took away from us.

"I'm sorry, I didn't mean to hurt anyone's feelings." I didn't turn to see Silas' face, instead, I watched after Laz, following them until they met up with Samara on the other side of the fence.

Silas ran his hand through his hair and turned to face me slowly. "You did nothing wrong, Athena. I, however, knew about Laz's feelings for you and acted on my own anyway." I saw the guilt etched on his face.

"I should probably go, I'm sorry for getting in the middle." Silas' eyes darkened and a devious smile spread across his lips. "You ok?" I asked, not sure I wanted to know the reason for his shifted mood.

"Just thinking about you in the middle." My face flushed and a positively juvenile giggle escaped my lips. I was definitely picturing that now too.

"I've gotta go, but thank you." Silas stepped forward, his scent invading my nostrils again, sending a shockwave directly to my center. His whispered voice aimed directly at my ear, and the skin touched by his breath erupted in goosebumps. "For showing us around." His lips landed on my neck, a brief kiss, but it was enough to draw a moan from my mouth. "And for the kiss." He planted another light kiss on my jaw. I felt my mouth fall open, and my eyes closed. "And for this." His lips found mine and his tongue quickly entered my open mouth. By the time I kissed him back, he was already pulling away. A nearly ravenous look on his face.

"You have my number," his eyes darkened. "Use it." He took a few steps away before I found my voice again.

"Are you all leaving town?" I called after him, attempting unsuccessfully to hide the desperation in my tone.

He kept walking but turned over his shoulder to send me a wink. "Not without you." And then he jogged, meeting up with the others on the other side of the fence in moments. Leaving me, completely stunned and positively turned on.

I watched them leave, my heart thumping in my chest.

What the hell just happened?

Ok, time to remember the facts. These four sexy strangers saved me from being raped last night. Then, they took care of me afterward. This morning after comforting me, they asked me to give them a tour of the town where two - kind of three? - of them flirted with me relentlessly. Then, like a girl with a schoolyard crush, I read a dirty book with them, out loud. I made out with the handsome tattooed one, like sucking each other's face off kind of makeout, and then the other one whose cock was against my leg earlier got extremely jealous.

I need to go home immediately. If only to relieve this burning ache between my legs with one of my many many toys. Something about them all makes me feel so sensual, so free. Like I have the right to take hold of those sinful desires I've only recently let myself feel again. I needed to get home and douse this flame immediately, but the thought of his lips on mine made it increasingly difficult to put one foot in front of the other. I glanced over my shoulder at the keep of the lighthouse and sighed warmly.

Panting breaths and grunts of exertion echoed in the keep when we reached the top. I helped Mom sit on the ground, her back up against the sturdy railing near the lantern's enclosure, then found myself a seat next to her. From our spot, we could look out over the water, watching the sun dance along the surface of the crystal ocean.

"You're out of shape," Mom teased breathlessly as I struggled to rein in my breathing. She had a smile on her lips, but I could see the energy dwindling with each passing second.

"This is a very tall lighthouse!" I complained gaspingly, wiping the sweat from my brow with the back of my palm. We sat in silence for several minutes watching the world in front of us carry on.

That's what it was going to do after all. Carry on. After she was gone, the sun would still rise, the waves would still crash against the rocks, the wind would still blow. No matter how her loss would rock my world, no matter how bleak and lonely I would feel. No matter how much I wish I could stop the moon from retreating every dawn and beg it to stop time. To stay in this moment forever. It wouldn't.

"Promise me something," my Mom said, her voice was tired, but she had a sort of authority about her that I respected. Even now, in her state, she could command a room.

"Anything," I assured her. She let her head tilt slightly until she was glancing at me, her eyes missing the glistening twinkle that I'd come to love from her stare.

"Promise me that you'll still try to live." A tear slipped from her eye and slid down her smooth skin. Smooth and fragile. Young. She was too young. I couldn't respond without breaking my own promise not to cry in front of her, so I just nodded. Her chest heaved with the exertion. "I'm sorry I couldn't protect you from everything." Her voice was sad, filled with guilt that I desperately wanted to erase from her soul. This guilt was mine to bear, not hers.

"Stop, you did everything you could." She shook her head, tears falling more readily. "You did."

"There are scars on your soul that I could have prevented, scars you will have for the rest of your life, and I hate that I can't kiss them better." I had to focus all of my energy on not letting the tears that were building in my eyes fall. She was exerting too much. Each word seemed to take too much and give too little.

I gently threw my arms around her and hugged her. She leaned her head into the crook of my neck, but her arms didn't reciprocate. She was too weak. I could hear her labored breathing from my close position to her chest.

"My soul would have had a lot more scars had you not been there to shield me, Mom," I whispered into her ear, speaking through clenched teeth, emotion cresting in my chest.

"You'll have to shield yourself now, love." It was barely a whisper, she struggled to force the words through her tired lips. When I pulled back from her face she had gotten even paler than before. Pain constricted in my heart. There wasn't much time left. I could see the sands of time running out in the dimness of her eyes.

"We should get you home," I said, jumping into action. "Grandma will want to talk to you." Tears were streaming now, I was completely unprepared to face this reality.

"Sit down, Athena," she demanded. I shook my head, preparing to pick her up and carry her back down the steps.

"We have to get you home, you should rest." I was rambling, I knew it. So did she. "I *need to call Grandma and the doctor. We shouldn't have come up here." I was panicking.*

"Athena." I paused, turning to look at my mother's face. It was an expression of acceptance, of submission. My breathing wouldn't slow.

"We have to go." She shook her head.

"Athena, please." A sob wrenched itself from my lips, a painful sound.

I crawled into the space next to her. "You knew when we came up here, didn't you?" I asked, choking on my sobs.

She nodded. I burrowed into her arms, laying my head on her chest. Pressing my ear against her skin so I could hear that heartbeat.

Thump. Thump.

"What about Grandma?" I cried.

"We said… our goodbyes already…now it's our turn," she said slowly. Using every ounce of energy she had left.

"I can't do this without you, Mom," I told her truthfully. Her breathing slowed.

"Yes you can, love." I could only hear her because I was so close to her. I gripped her in my arms, as tight as I could without hurting her.

Thump… Thump.

"I love you. I love you. I love you." I murmured into her chest.

Thump.

"I love you."

Thump.

"I love you."

…

"I love you."

With a dazed look over my shoulder at the lighthouse, I silently thank Silas for giving me another happy memory here, one that could soften the blow of my final minutes here with her.

"I love you, Mom," I whispered, feeling the weight of grief on my soul lighten with each step away.

ORPHEUS

TEN

"I understand that you are booked for the season, but I'd urge you to find me a listing." I was a businessman at heart. Negotiations, acquisitions, and analyzing risks. I think I was similar as a human, but I'm not entirely sure anymore. One of the curses - or I guess in some cases like Samara - blessings, of our second life, is that after a while the details get fuzzy, and you start to forget the mortal life you led, the people in it, the kind of person you were. The birth of your second life becomes the only one that matters. It takes a long time to dissipate, longer if it was particularly impactful, so unfortunately for Samara, her wicked past will still loom over her for a while longer. But I remember being quite detail oriented, and skilled in the art of negotiating from the very beginning of my second life, so I can assume that was a skill I picked up from my previous existence.

"I'm sorry, sir." The realtor's shrill voice grated against my subconscious. My fists clenched at my sides at her words. She had her platinum hair pulled back in a tight ponytail that pulled her skin taut, and her shapeless form was draped in a tight burgundy skirt and jacket set. Her feet were stuffed into ridiculously uncomfortable-looking heels. "We have no homes available for the season."

I forced myself not to roll my eyes before reaching into my suit jacket and pulling out a large stack of cash. I've spent long enough in this world to know that when money talks, people listen.

"I will buy out another renter's contract, and give them a sizable donation so they can find new accommodations." The blonde's eyebrows shot up and she pursed her painted-red lips.

"Paying in cash?" Her gaze scanned me. "I think it is my duty to remind you that we do not stand for any sort of illicit activity in any of our rental properties." I couldn't control my eye roll then.

"Ma'am." I didn't miss her wince at the word. Or the feeling of embarrassment flooding her emotions. So she was one of those women who loathed the idea of growing older. Noted. Time to shift tactics. "Miss," I started, leaning forward on the counter until I could feel her heat. A sudden rush of lustful energy began radiating off of her, but to her credit, her face remained emotionless. "I'm sorry, I can see I've wasted your time." I darted my tongue out to wet my bottom lip and saw her eyes follow the movement. Her chest moved with deeper heaving breaths as she watched me, and struggled against the very potent and very real feelings of desire that were building in her.

I couldn't stop the part of me that unconsciously differentiated how this woman's rush of arousal felt in comparison to Athena's. From a completely objective standpoint, there was no contest. Where this blonde's emotion felt abrupt and harsh, like grabbing the handle of a hot pan without a glove, Athena's felt like a warm fire slowly building to a climax.

I did not just think of Athena and the word climax in the same sentence. I need to stop letting Laz, Samara, and Silas' emotions around her influence me.

"We have a home near the pier, right on the beach, it's booked for the season but the tenants usually only spend their weekends there." I leaned forward again until I was well and truly in her space, I studied her carefully, masking my face to seem like the most interested person she's ever spoken to.

"Do you think they would mind?" I asked innocently. She smiled, her face flushing at the undivided attention I was giving her.

"I think I can make it work," she giggled, wrapping a small strand of blonde around her index finger.

"You're a saint," I nearly hissed the word, but she fell for it, despite my clear indignation at the ridiculous claim.

"I'll work on getting the paperwork, you just wait right here." She winked and took off, dragging her potent and not-at-all-alluring scent of arousal with her.

I stood up straight as she disappeared behind the office door. I hated resorting to my charms to get what I needed, but with so much on the line and so little time to formulate this plan, I didn't have time to follow through on anything quite as… intricate as I would have liked.

I turned to face the front of the office, a full wall of windows, and a single glass door. A Shockgrove Vacation Rentals decal was plastered on the surface and blocked some of the sun rays that spilled through the glass.

I waited impatiently for a few moments for the blonde to return with my rental information. The sound of her heels clicking against the tile surface had me turning back to the desk, fixing my smile in place.

"Ok, we just need some of your information and we can get this all set up." She slid some documents across the desk to me. She held out a pen, waiting for me to grab it. As I did she purposefully brushed her hand against mine. I had to fight against pulling my skin from hers as she touched me. She smiled meekly.

I got to work on the paperwork, utilizing one of the many pseudonyms I've adopted to avoid any paper trails. David Green was a business executive from New York, he had been purchasing and distributing underage pornography. We decided the world was better off without him. His blood kept us fed for a few weeks, and his ID kept us hidden for longer.

"So," she started, glancing down at the paperwork in front of me. "David." She smiled at the name. "Are you here with a wife or a girlfriend?" I didn't respond at first. On one hand, I didn't want her to feel like I had played her, although I most definitely had. On the other hand, I had no intention of following through on any silent promises our eyes made to each other as I charmed her into getting me what I needed. I had to play this delicately.

"Actually, I…" My words were cut off by the most intense wave of emotions I had ever felt in my entire existence. My eyes widened as I looked at the realtor, the only other person in my vicinity. But this feeling wasn't coming from her. I doubled over as another wave of sheer panic hit me.

"Are you ok?" I vaguely heard the woman asking. I waved her off.

"I just need some air, I apologize," I gritted through clenched teeth. "I'll be right back." I stumbled out of the office and into the midday air, as my breathing became difficult.

Panic.

A lot of it.

I bent at the waist, a hand to my heart, I felt phantom beats from a heart that wasn't mine, rapid and violent as I fought against the wave of crashing anxiety. The sting of the sun's light as it touched my face was a mild inconvenience compared to the brutal weight of this emotional barrage. I looked around, thrashing painfully looking for the culprit. The person whose emotions were so vivid and so close that I felt them this deeply.

I was alone. There was nobody else roaming the empty streets.

My back hit the brick wall behind me, settling under the shade of an awning giving my tender skin a moment to recover from the burn, as I struggled to regain a semblance of composure. There was no explanation for this feeling, no reason that I was experiencing something this painful when nobody was around. Instantly, the thought came to me. What if something happened to my coven? I've never felt their emotions this strongly, and certainly never from this far away, but that doesn't mean it couldn't. Fumbling for my phone, I rang Samara.

She picked up after four rings.

"Orpheus," her voice was strained, I couldn't read her emotions from here, but if I had to guess I'd say she was worried about something.

"What's wrong?" I asked, masking the current vicious emotion that continued to swim around my head.

"It's fine. I think." I waited for her to explain. Had Laz or Silas been hurt? The tight feeling in my chest was slowly receding, but the cool embrace of the panic's hold on my heart was present, and I'm sure it would remain that way for quite some time.

"What happened?" My breathing had returned to a relatively normal cadence and despite the sweat gleaming on my forehead, I was feeling as if I was collected.

"We're at the lighthouse, I think Athena may have had a panic attack." My breathing ceased again, my entire body going frigidly still.

"How long ago?" I asked through clenched teeth.

"Just now, although she seems to be settling down," I heard the concern in Samara's voice for Athena, but I didn't have time to analyze it.

I glanced toward the lighthouse, it was barely visible from my position this far inland. It must be a coincidence. It has to be. There's no reason why I would feel her panic, not from that distance, and certainly not that strongly.

Back at the diner this morning I had felt her guilt and her fear, but had it been any stronger than normal? I don't know. My head was spinning, my skin was tender from the sunlight and my chest was tight as I cleared my throat.

"I found us a place since Silas insists we stay put."

"Text me the address and we'll meet you there." After issuing my agreement, I shot off a text with the address of our new rental, then sauntered back into the office to complete the paperwork.

I needed to focus on our safety, our plans, and our survival. I didn't have time to worry about if it was her panic that I felt, and if so…why?

I didn't have time to think about why the idea of Athena in a panic was sending murderous thoughts through my head.

SILAS

ELEVEN

Her scent was still strong, each time the wind caressed me, a cloud of her minty aroma wafted up to my nostrils and I hardened instantly. Her kiss was fucking wicked. I'd never felt so out of control before. Never felt so overcome by mindless attraction.

And yet, still no mate bond.

Although, she didn't bleed today.

To our kind, you must scent someone's blood for the mate bond to snap into place. So logically, last night, when she was bleeding after her encounter with that piece of shit, it should have happened. It didn't.

So why, even with this impossible-to-refute proof staring back at me, was I so fucking positive that this woman was mine? How was it that my entire body, every fucking nerve ending sang when I was around her if she wasn't my mate? How am I already missing her after leaving her only five minutes ago, if I don't belong to her?

Mate or not, I am Athena's. And she is mine.

My eyes drift to my side, Laz had been quietly walking alongside me. Their anger was pretty potent. I didn't need Orpheus and his ability to confirm that

I shouldn't have kissed her, not without talking to Laz first, but they knew the moment that they walked away to retrieve her bag that they were giving me permission. Whether they knew it or not. Still, I couldn't help the guilt that was tugging at my subconscious. Samara walked ahead of us, her eyes scanning the street names, leading us to the address that Orpheus sent over.

"Laz…" I started, but they put up a hand.

"Not out here, ok? I am barely keeping myself together as it is, I don't need to shift and go all Dracula on your ass in broad daylight in front of our new neighbors." I smirked at that. I've been with The Wanderers for a long time. I have seen Laz when they are angry, like irredeemably angry, and that usually manifests itself in a sort of quiet simmering rage. Silence before the storm and all that. So the fact that they were speaking to me at all at that moment told me that I had not broken us beyond repair.

I watched my friend as Samara turned down a driveway. Trying to place myself in their shoes. If I had walked away to get her bag, would she have kissed them? Did she feel the same pull toward Laz as she did for me? If she had, and I'd walked back to see them locked in a passionate embrace would I have been able to stop myself from tearing them off of her? I'm not sure. The pent-up rage in their closed fist at their side told me that I was one wrong word away from having to spar with my friend. I pushed that thought away and followed Samara. There was a rental car in the driveway. Smart, wouldn't want the neighbors to think we run everywhere. Orpheus thinks of everything.

The moment we stepped through the front door and it closed behind us, Laz was on me. I fell to the ground and they caged me down with their body. Their hands gripped my throat with as much ill intent as they could manage. It was child's play truly in comparison to other fights I've been in, but I let them take and keep the upper hand.

"You son of a bitch!" Laz pushed down on my windpipe, not enough to do any real damage, which is how I knew that we were ok and they just needed to air their frustrations. I let them.

"What the fuck is going on?" Orpheus called from the stairwell.

"Silas kissed Athena, and Laz is gonna kill him," Samara rattled off, unimpressed, but I noticed a slight edge to her jawline. Like she wasn't too happy about my alleged indiscretion either.

"For fuck's sake."

Laz slammed their fist into my face, and it hurt, don't get me wrong, but it felt like any actual hatred was long gone and this was coming from a place of pain. "Get up you two, now." Laz graced me with one more hit across the jaw before dismounting and standing. They stalked off through the back door, the one that led to a pretty solid-looking patio, and down onto the beach. We watched after them for a moment before Orpheus sighed.

"Nice place," I said with a low whistle, massaging my throbbing jaw. The interior was bright, with that beachy nautical vibe that New Englanders love so much. Blue walls and starfish decor, hardwood floors, and a huge living room. The space was furnished with burlap and oak furniture that looked the appropriate amount of rich and rustic, no doubt so the bastards who rent this place in the summer feel like they're doing something special with their lives.

There was a spiral staircase that led up to a second floor, a balcony overlooking the living space here with vaulted ceilings. I only had a briefest thought of fucking Athena against that railing before Orpheus gripped my shoulder.

"So…you kissed her," he spoke with a slightly accusatory tone. "Anything?"

I shook my head, and he rolled his eyes, groaning as he walked away.

"She didn't bleed, Orpheus." He tossed his hands up before sinking onto the couch next to Samara.

"You could have bit her lip or something," He offered and I couldn't stop the smile that played on my lips. My tongue ran across my bottom lip and the piercing there, remembering how it felt to have her tongue do the same. Relishing in the memory of her teeth closing around my lip, claiming it as hers.

"She beat me to it." I fell back into the armchair that sat across from the couch and smiled at Orpheus. Samara's eyes flicked to my lips and I knew she wasn't thinking of kissing me, but rather imagining the person who had.

"You need to figure this shit out sooner rather than later. We have a place to stay, but I don't intend to make this an extended pitstop." I nodded. I knew the risks and I understood intimately why the Hunters could never be able to find us again.

Alora was my best friend. Samara of course fell head over heels for the girl, but she was my friend from when we were humans. Losing her was hard on us all, but it nearly killed Samara and I. Those Hunters will never get the chance to do that to another one of us, ever again.

"I know. I will. I'm not unaware of the risks here." He nodded, satisfied with my answer. He was right. I was going to have to get a whiff of Athena's blood soon. But I needed to wait until I was sure that toxic shit that that fuckwad from last night gave her was completely out of her system. I needed to be sure, to be absolutely positive. If I was going to leave this place without her, I needed a damn good reason.

"For what it's worth," Orpheus started, leaning forward to rest his elbows on his knees and clasp his hands together in front of him. "I can sense it - how you feel about her." My breath caught in my throat. He knew we hated when he read our emotions. "And before you go getting your panties in a twist, I'm not reading you intentionally, it's just that strong." I smiled then. I knew how I felt about her, but it was nice to have someone validate that it feels just as earth-shattering from the outside. "I can understand why, with emotions that strong, you are so focused on discovering if there's a bond here. I've never seen you feel this way for someone before." He paused before standing and walking toward the back door. He turned slightly then, a wistful smile on his lips, glancing over at the door that Laz left through, but not before tossing a slight look toward Samara on the couch. "If it changes anything…they feel it too."

I ran a hand through my hair, combing it out of its bind at the back of my head and letting it fall freely around my face while releasing a deep sigh. Of course, Laz felt this way. Did Orpheus intend to look at Samara? Could she be feeling similarly? She's always been so reserved with her feelings. It took decades for her to make a move with Alora. Shit, we were both going to need the time to determine if she was our mate. Athena was going to change everything. I just hoped we'd be able to handle it. As a coven. As The Wanderers.

A slight buzz from my pocket had my entire demeanor shifting. A total of five people had this number. Seeing as two of them were currently in my periphery and one of them wanted nothing to do with me right now. My options were down to two. My body relaxed when I saw a local number. Her number.

ATHENA: So what do I get?

I shook my head, scrolling up to see if I'd missed another message. Something that makes more sense.

SILAS: What do you get?

I typed back my response, quickly.

ATHENA: Yeah…What do I get?

My eyebrows furrowed as I typed back.

SILAS: For what, bookworm?

I smiled at her nickname, and the memory it elicited. God, what I'd give to go back to her shop alone and read each dirty scene in that entire place and reenact every single one with her.

ATHENA: You told me to use your phone number.

I tilted my head in confusion, watching as the dots appeared again as she typed.

ATHENA: I followed orders.

My cock twitched in my pants, and I bit down on my lip to avoid the moan that wanted to escape. I stood and raced up the steps toward the bedrooms, I found an empty one with pale green walls and a king-sized bed facing double balcony doors by the time she responded again.

ATHENA: So what do I get in return?

I threw the door closed behind me and nearly sprawled out on the bed typing back. I had half a mind to say 'whatever the fuck you want,' which was technically true, but that's not the game she wanted to play right now. And I was more than willing to give her what she wanted.

SILAS: You did follow orders, I guess you do deserve a reward don't you?

A giddy excitement was budding in my chest, and my cock was hard, tenting my pants. I unbuttoned them and slid them off, leaving my boxers for the time being. If only just to avoid touching myself and exploding before I wanted to.

ATHENA: Yes. Please.

That fucking word. I was going to make her scream it the next time I saw her.

SILAS: Good girl. You know how much I love that word on your fucking lips.

When she didn't immediately respond, I worried that I may have taken the game too far too fast, we only met last night for Christ's sake and didn't even speak till this morning after all. When my phone buzzed again I sat up against the headboard with a jolt.

ATHENA: If I say it again, what will you give me?

And down go the boxers. With one hand, I type my message back, letting my other finally touch my aching cock, stroking it to offer some relief.

SILAS: Say it once, and I'll kiss your lips. Say it twice and I'll take your nipples into my mouth. Three times and I'll devour your pussy with my tongue. But four times, that's when I spear you with my cock and fuck you until you can't breathe.

I was panting, breathing raggedly as I stroked myself to the thought of following through on my promises. Her next text came quickly.

ATHENA: Please.

I smiled as the bubble returned.

ATHENA: Please.

And again.

ATHENA: Please.

I nearly came from seeing the text bubble appear once more.

ATHENA: Please.

I struggled for only a moment to text back, while holding my cock in one hand before I gave up and called her. She didn't answer for a few agonizing rings, but on the fifth ring, her sultry voice echoed in my ear.

"Hi, Silas." I knew right then that I'd give nearly everything to have her say my name again. I was in trouble. I wanted to tell her how I felt, tell her how I never wanted to be without her. But I was playing a role in a game that we both wanted to play.

"Put me on speaker," I barely recognized my lust-filled voice as I gave the rushed command.

"Ok." She replied and I heard a slight rustling, then the sound amplified telling me that she had once again followed my orders.

"Good. Now undress for me. Completely," I ordered. I heard a slight moan escape from her lips on the other line and I thanked whatever devil gave me my new and improved hearing because I heard every glorious fucking note of it. "Tell me what you're doing. Explain it to me." I stroked my cock, slowly just enough to satisfy the primal need burning within me, but holding back enough to prolong this moment.

"I'm removing my dress." I closed my eyes and pictured the grey t-shirt dress she wore earlier. It fit her frame well, showing off her tits and ass like the taunting delicious features they were. "Now I'm removing my bra." I smiled but noticed the slight timidness in her tone.

"Describe it to me." There was an ounce of hesitation on her end of the line and my fingers stilled. "Athena, I love this game and I want to play it with you. But if you need me to stop I will." I heard a sigh, relief perhaps, coming from her side. "Just say 'blood' and we stop, ok?"

"Ok." She replied, the sensual tone returning to her voice.

"Let me hear you say it baby girl so I know you can." I felt like I was alight, burning from the inside out.

"I will say blood if I need you to stop."

"That's my fucking girl," I growled, and my hand resumed its torturous stroking of my cock.

"My bra is black, it matches my underwear." I moaned, loudly. I hope Orpheus and Samara had the good sense to leave the house, or at least throw some headphones on. Or hell, maybe they want to listen. Hear how I make her feel.

"Take them both off. I need you naked for me." I heard her movement confirming she was listening to my demands.

"I'm naked." She was shy, but there was something so sexy about that. She wanted this as badly as I did, but she wasn't sure she should let herself have it. Well, I was about to show her that she deserved every second of this and so much more.

"Show me," I strained, pressing the video chat button on the phone. I knew I should resist. To let the first time I see her like this be in front of me when I can touch her, feel her. But I couldn't. I needed her. I needed to see her, now.

She answered the video call and my heart would have stopped had it not already. Her hair was loose hanging around her face, framing her blushed cheeks perfectly. Her green eyes were filled with the same desire I saw at the lighthouse and her body… her fucking perfect body. Her breasts were thick and perfectly rounded and the hardened peaks were begging for my mouth. From this angle, I couldn't see past the soft planes of her stomach. I smiled at her with a devious smirk.

"You're being very good for me, Athena." I watched as her bottom lip was sucked between her teeth at that. I didn't miss the way her breath caught or the way she pressed her thighs together. "Set your phone down so I can see you. Lay back on the bed and spread your legs for me. Do it now, Athena." She nodded, a stunning picture, and did as I said. As she laid back and spread her legs, offering me the first glimpse of her perfect little cunt. I stroked my cock faster, pretending it was her I was thrusting into and not my hand.

"Fuck, baby girl. I can see how wet you are from here. Have you touched your little cunt yet, or were you wanting for me?" It was hard to keep this composed image of a dominant man when all I wanted was to sink to my knees below her where I belonged and taste her.

"I was waiting," she confessed.

"Touch yourself for me, Athena." I watched with rapt attention as her hands trailed along her breasts, slowly and carefully. Her fingertips brushed against her nipples just enough to send a jolt of pleasure through her. I grasped at my balls, matching her burst of euphoria with my own. Her hands traveled lower until they were nearly where I needed them. "That's it, baby. Touch your clit." She did and I nearly detonated on the spot at the sound she made as her fingers found her most sensitive spot. "Fuck baby, that sound is going to kill me one day." Her head lolled back and she continued her exploration of that bundle of nerves. I licked my lips to keep from begging her to come sit on them.

"Do you use any toys, Athena?" Her eyes snapped back toward the screen, her flushed skin looked delicious next to her mused red hair. She nodded. "Yes, sir." I fucking choked.

"Hell, baby. Say that again." I rasped through clenched teeth, holding on to my composure with a fucking thread.

"Yes. Sir." She separated each word letting her tongue really taste them. I was going to get that tattooed on my fucking skin. Right over the place where my fucking heart used to beat because if it was still alive I had no doubt it would be hers.

"Grab your favorite one." She blushed deeper but didn't argue. She rolled out of view for a moment and I was devastated at the loss until she returned and spread herself wide for me once more. She held up the purple wand. It had a bud on the inside, clearly built for insertion and clit stimulation all at once. "Put it in your mouth, Athena, get it nice and wet for me." Something flashed across her expression briefly and panic threatened to seize my heart, but she didn't say the word, and the look was gone almost as quickly as it had come. She raised the toy to her mouth and pressed it inside, not without giving me a show with her tongue. I groaned and stroked faster. I was going to fuck her so hard the next time I see her, nothing in the world could stop me. Not even Laz. She sucked on the toy as if it were a cock, her eyes closing as she groaned around it, the wet sounds making me feel fucking powerless against her.

"Fuck yourself, Athena. Fuck yourself the way you want me to fuck you." She gasped, and slowly removed the toy from her mouth. She dragged the tip of it down her torso, torturously close to her wet hot heat. When she slid the toy into her cunt, I sucked in a breath so deep I felt it in my core. She moaned loudly and I wondered if her house was secluded or if people would hear how well she took that toy for me. I didn't know which answer I wanted.

She held the device deep within her and smiled sinfully at me and then pressed a button. The vibrations might as well have been on my own cock, because I came with a roar as I watched her squirm beneath the movement of the toy. Her head fell back as she pressed the toy deeper and cried out as it stimulated her. "Fuck, that's it, baby." It didn't even matter that I had just come, my cock was already twitching back to life for her.

Then there was a knock on her door. She stopped, pulling the toy from her quickly and sliding off the bed embarrassed. I groaned in frustration that someone had interrupted my little game. Then an idea occurred to me and I felt the devious smile on my lips deepen.

"Do you have a robe, baby girl?" She looked at the screen, a deep blush of embarrassment on her face.

"Yes." She answered, timidly.

"Yes, what?" I goaded her. She bit her bottom lip.

"Yes, sir." I nearly came again.

"Put it on." She did, still following orders, I see. She deserves a reward. "Now slide that toy back into your wet little pussy." Her eyes widened in shock.

"What?"

"Put that toy back in your cunt, then go answer the door. Take me with you." She watched the screen like she was contemplating saying our safe word, and I would have let her. I know I was still playing the game, but if she wanted out, then we were out. She licked her lips and then nodded, slowly opening her robe just enough to give me a view of her sliding the purple toy back into her slick folds. She moaned and then closed the robe, hiding the evidence. She picked me up and took me with her to the door. I heard her frustrated grunts with each step as the toy stimulated her clit. I stayed quiet as she opened the door.

"Laz!" I jolted upright, leaning forward to try and see. She had slipped me into the pocket of the robe, so all I saw was faint light coming through a grey fabric. She was embarrassed, I felt it in her tone. She was in nothing but a light robe, because of my stupid game. I hated myself.

"Oh, I'm sorry. I didn't mean to…I um.." I could hear Laz's trepidation. On one hand, a very underdressed beautiful woman was in front of them, on the other, she hadn't been that way for their sake. I wondered if they would be upset to learn of the little game we had been playing. Once again the guilt I had felt earlier began to gnaw at me. If Orpheus was right, and Laz was feeling the same way I was, then I know I would raise hell. Laz would be the type to simmer in their anger, to hold it in until there was an explosion unlike any we've seen before. "I can come back… I'm so sorry." They were scrambling, anxious. Pulled between their desire for her and their desire to be courteous. To hell with being courteous. That's where the two of us differ. I can't say with any ounce of certainty that I wouldn't have already sealed her lips in a kiss had I been the one at the door.

"No, it's ok. I um… was just." She was nervous. I could hear that clear as day. There was a slight excitement to her tone too. When you've spent as long as I have learning to decipher tones, to replicate their mannerisms, you learn what people are saying when they aren't saying anything at all. And right now, Athena was saying that she was turned on, and I think the person in front of her had just as much to do with it as I had.

Jealousy flashed for a moment, but only a moment. Then a different kind of resolve flooded me. Laz was one of the best people I've ever known. One of the most genuine souls I'd met in the eternity I've been alive. Athena would never know a better person or a more attentive partner.

Could I share? Could I willingly give a piece of what I believe to be my mate to someone else?

The answer should have been no. The answer would have been no if I'd been asked it even an hour ago. But Orpheus had been sure to tell me how strongly he knew I felt for her and he needed me to know that Laz felt the same. Maybe even Samara as well. The same burning passion, the same clear and honest pull to her, they feel it too. Laz needs to know if she is their mate, just as badly as I do.

But if I'm going to share, I'm going to watch.

ǅLAZ

TWELVE

After leaving Silas with a parting gift of my fist in his face, I stormed out of the beach house and down onto the shore. I didn't stop when I hit the water, I simply turned and let my feet walk while my mind struggled to get ahold of my heart. Sure, throughout the many many years that we have been a coven we've gotten into arguments, and even punched each other a few times, but this was different. I wanted to hurt Silas, even though I knew I couldn't. The entire walk home, every word he said only reminded me of the way his lips claimed hers. The way his hands explored her body and pulled her to him. I had never felt jealousy as potent or raw as I did then. I wanted to rush to them, pull Silas off of her body, and take his place. To finish what we dangerously began at the bookstore.

Sometimes I think I'm too cautious for my own good. I am the type of person who sees something I want, then I spend the next several days, months even, researching and understanding it. Laying out a list of pros and cons, and analyzing if this is something that I can afford to pursue. Then and only then do I go for it. Spontaneous, I am not.

But Athena makes me want to be. She makes me want to throw caution to the wind and dive headfirst into the unknown, as long as she's by my side. I think that if someone forces you to change who you are to be with them then that is toxic and dangerous…but if you find someone who makes you want to change, makes you *want* to grow and learn and be a better person then that's fate. I'm that fool who watches Grease and says that both of those people wanted to be something different and were looking for the excuse to go for it. Sandy wanted a wild side, and Danny wanted a soft side. They brought that out in each other. Will they last? Who knows. But what changed between them, how they grew because of each other? That was fate.

That has to mean something. She has to mean something to me.

Before I realized what was happening, my feet had turned down her driveway. Orpheus unknowingly nabbed us a place only a few streets away from her. At least I think it was unknowingly.

I stopped at the end of the drive, watching the blue house with fascination. Now that I've met her, now that I've talked to her, it was even clearer why this house seemed like her. She was sweet and timid. But colorful and vibrant. Cozy. Like home.

I knew I should turn away and return home. There was no reason why I should be here right now. It was an invasion of privacy.

Then I heard it.

Soft, sweet moans wafted through the air. Not loud enough for any human ear to catch, but I heard it. I heard it all. Her breathy whimpers sent a shockwave directly to my core.

Near mindless, I took a step forward before I was able to regain composure and shake off the hooks she unknowingly had in me. I should leave. I should turn around.

I couldn't.

Caution to the wind. I walked forward, savoring each delicious moan that came from her home. But while I was focusing on her sweet voice, I heard another, and a chill ran down my spine. Silas. His dark and commanding tone was coming through a speaker. I was half tempted to call him and interrupt his little call with our girl. I shook my head. *Our girl?* I brushed my hands down my face, contemplating leaving again for the third time. Then I knocked.

I heard her stumble about the room, and I tried not to listen to Silas' words, afraid they'd only make me angry and waited for her to arrive at the door.

Her flushed skin was the most beautiful thing I'd ever seen. Her red hair was loose around her shoulders, tousled just enough to tell me she had been in an intimate position.

"Oh, I'm sorry. I didn't mean to... I um...I can come back. I'm so sorry." I averted my gaze despite every fiber of my being that begged me to stare, to soak up every moment of the time when she stood before me.

She drew her robe closed tighter and blushed deeply. I took a slow step back. Tell me to stay, Athena. Tell me to stay, please.

"No, it's ok. I um… was just." I smiled, turning my head back to look at her.

"I fear I may have caught you in an intimate moment," I said, smirking. I wasn't the best flirt, but I'd seen Silas and Samara engage in the act enough to replicate a bit.

She giggled, actually giggled, and I found myself grinning like an idiot at the musical sound. "This is embarrassing," she confessed.

"Do you want Laz to join our game, baby girl?" Silas' voice echoed from the pocket of her robe. So he was listening?

Game?

I watched her carefully as she fumbled with the phone in her pocket, her pale skin a deep crimson color.

"Uh, what?" She held the phone up to look at the screen. So it was a video call, then. What had he gotten to see from my delicious-looking Athena?

"Do you want Laz to play too?" Silas asked, his voice nearly unrestrained. I didn't have to look at the screen to see that he was nearing a shift. His eyes would be bloodshot. Hell, just seeing her in this robe had me nearly following suit. I can only guess what he's had the pleasure of experiencing and how much willpower it's taken him to last this long.

Athena glanced up at me, her green eyes shining with lust as she looked up at me through dark eyelashes. It's been a while since I had a heart, but if I still did, I knew it would be racing as I waited for her answer.

Silas was offering me a chance with her. Sharing. I'd never thought about something like that before, especially not with my coven, who are basically my family. But at this moment, I let the possibility swirl around my mind and it made my erection stand at attention.

"Yes," she answered, timidly, yet with a sort of barely restrained desire.

"Yes, what baby?" Silas asked and my eyes burned into hers.

"Yes, sir." She spoke to him, but her eyes were on mine. The words were for him, but the gaze, the desire. That was mine.

She was like a present I wanted to unwrap. I didn't need another invitation, I pushed through the door, thankful that she had already invited me in last night because right now I didn't care to wait for another second to claim her lips with mine. I pressed my mouth to hers and swallowed the gasp that she released before sinking into my hold. Her lips drank at me hungrily but slowly building like a fire, and I smiled against her mouth as my hands held her face to mine. I had plenty of time to explore her body, but right now I wanted her lips.

Her hands clasped around my neck, holding me firmly in place as her tongue begged for entry to my mouth. It was a passionate kiss, tender. We didn't feast on each other's mouths like animals, we didn't tear at each other's clothes - although my hands twitched to do just that. Instead, we kissed like lovers who were embracing the moment, living in it. Existing in this perfect instance with each other.

"Ah ah ah." I heard Silas from the phone that was now clasped in her hand behind my head. Athena pulled back, smiling shyly at me, and pulled her phone off to the side so that we both could see Silas on the screen, and he could see us.

"If we're going to play this game we need to set some ground rules. Take Laz to your room, baby girl." If I had heard him say those words at any other time I might have rolled my eyes, but here in the thick cloud of lust with Athena's body pressed against mine, I eagerly awaited his next command.

She pulled her body from mine, and I desperately missed her warmth. Grabbing my hand she led me through the living room toward her room. I smiled to myself when I saw the spot on her mattress where I sat last night, watching over her. How quickly I cared for this girl should have worried me, the way Orpheus was worried, but I couldn't care less how hard I fell for this human. Her red hair bounced with each delicious swing of her hips and I was about to lose my restraint. She moved to prop her phone on a shelf. From where it sat, you could see the entire bed. I found myself thinking about what she and Silas were up to when I arrived, and instead of jealousy coursing through me at that thought, it was curiosity, pure and unbridled passionate curiosity.

"Tell Laz our safeword, baby girl," Laz ordered. I flicked my eyes to Athena who was standing at the foot of the bed, an almost shy look on her face. She glanced down at the floor as she spoke.

"Blood." I groaned at the word on her lips, tossing Silas a look I'm sure he could decipher.

"Good girl." It didn't take my vampiric senses to tell how those two little words affected her. It was fascinating to see how Silas had fit so clearly into the role of a dominant personality with her. I was eager to see what my role would be with her. I'd be just about anything for this woman, do just about anything to see her blush at me the way she blushed at his words.

"Take off your robe." Silas sounded calm, collected, and dominant, but I knew all his tells, I knew how close he was to detonation. I wasn't far behind him.

She turned her eyes from the screen to me, smiling shyly before moving her hands to the collar of the grey robe. I moved to grip her wrist, stopping her momentarily. She looked up at me with confusion.

"Let me go first," I offered, and a dark desire crossed her face. "Is that ok, Sir?" I asked Silas. I don't know what possessed me to do so, but something told me that if I wanted this to continue I needed to play the game. Honestly, I wanted to. I noticed the surprise on both of their faces but didn't let it deter me.

"Yes. Undress for her, Laz. Put on a fucking show." And so I did. I took my time removing my shirt, buttoning each button as her eyes trailed my fingers. I even let my fingertips trail across my bare abdomen on my way down to my pants. Removing them and my briefs in one sweep. My length stood tall for her. All for her. Well, maybe a little for the game too. Not that I was attracted to Silas or anything, but I think I liked taking orders from him. Athena's eyes swept my body appreciatively, a coy smirk claiming her lips as she took in my endowment. I was girthier than most, I bet she was picturing how it would feel inside of her. So was I.

"Your turn, baby girl." Athena sensually dropped the shoulders of her robe one at a time, offering me just a quick glimpse of the skin beneath before dropping it all to the ground. As the robe pooled around her feet, I took an involuntary step closer. My shift right under the surface.

"Close your eyes, Athena," Silas ordered quickly and she followed quicker. I tossed a look at the screen and he shared a look with me, a silent check-in. I needed to be sure I was under control. I took a deep breath, feeling my fangs settle and the cloud dissipate, then nodded to him, the hesitancy from his face was replaced with his mask of dominance. "Show Laz our little toy." My eyes turned to her again, watching as she sat down on the bed and slowly, one leg at a time, spread her legs for me offering me the perfect view of her perfect sex, currently stretched by a purple toy.

"Athena. You are stunning." I whispered to her and I heard her soft moan tell me she was listening despite her eyes remaining shut.

"Do you want a taste, Laz?" I swallowed deeply, Silas knew as well as I did what else I desperately wanted to taste right now, but damn, her sweet arousal would be enough.

"Yes," I said, but it was barely more than a whisper, my breath was shallow in her narcotic presence.

"Yes, what, Laz?" Silas was lost to his own senses. I was too. And I loved it.

"Yes, Sir," I tossed back over my shoulder, my eyes stayed trained on the gorgeous woman spread before me like my own personal feast.

"Then do it."

ATHENA

THIRTEEN

Who the hell was I right now? Not the timid, scared, shattered girl I'd been for the last decade of my life. For so long I let that one horrific night cast its shadow on every day of my existence. But not here, not with these two. When I got home after the tour and the kiss, I grabbed my favorite vibrator - the one currently stretching me - like I had every other time I was turned on in the slightest. They were safer than being with a partner. Especially men. I didn't take the risk, I didn't give in to their advances. The few times I did manage to open myself and my legs for someone new, the memory was so vicious and deep that I wasn't in the moment. Not really. But right now? With Silas' words guiding me, with Laz's eyes on my naked body? I felt powerful. Like a woman who deserved passion. And no matter how many times I looked into either of their eyes, I didn't see *his*.

So when I went to grab that vibrator, instead I grabbed my phone and took the first step to take back my life. Now here I was, Silas' thick voice giving me commands, ordering me to do dirty things for him. A familiar thing, but this time…I knew I had a way out. That was the clear and honest difference. There was trust here. Something that was missing the last time. Something *he* never cared to build with me. Something I had with these strangers the moment I heard what they all did for me last night.

Laz's body was close to mine, I felt the cold air radiating off of them. How were they so cool when I was burning up, an absolute inferno burning within me?

With my eyes closed, my other senses were on high alert. Paying attention to every little movement. Noticing the way Laz's breath hitched as they sank to their knees in front of me. The way Silas groaned his approval. The slick sound of Laz pulling my vibrator from its place inside of me. I leaned back on my elbows and let my head fall back as I relished the feel of the toy rubbing against my walls. Once it was gone, I immediately missed the feeling of being stretched, but the loss was replaced with anticipation quickly when I felt their breath on my clit. I'm not sure I could ever be more turned on than I was at this very moment.

"Tell me how she tastes, Laz."

I lied. Definitely more turned on right now.

Before I could whine, begging for their tongue to ravish me, they closed their mouth over my clit and sucked. I screamed in pleasure as a jolt made my entire body tighten. They let their tongue take the lead then, dragging it through my folds, absolutely drenched with my arousal. They drank my taste like it was the greatest thing they'd ever had on their tongue. Their appreciative moans against my sex had me bucking off the bed. Their strong hands came to my waist and pressed me back down, holding me in place to endure this pleasurable torture.

"You taste like fine wine," they growled against my clit before swirling their tongue around it again. I gasped, my mouth hanging open. "Like the finest wine that's ever graced my tongue," They speared me, entering me as far as they could and I gripped at their hair, pulling their face closer. I needed more. I needed them deeper. Harder. I just needed.

I'd never experienced such blind euphoria. They slipped a finger into my folds, stretching me as they feasted on my clit like they were ravenous.

"Make her come," Silas demanded through breathless pants. I dared to open my eyes and catch a glimpse of the scene before me. Laz was buried between my legs, their eyes closed as they savored me. My eyes flicked to the screen to see Silas' dark eyes watching hungrily. His breathing was uneven, and I saw his shoulder moving in slow steady movements. He was touching himself. He was enjoying the show.

So was I.

"Yes, Sir," Laz whispered against my sex before they slipped a second finger inside of me, curling them slightly to reach that perfect spot that had my whole body shaking. I was on the edge.

I felt Laz's teeth grace my clit with a wicked promise and I toppled off the ledge. My thighs tightened around their head, holding them to me until the last wracks of my orgasm had had their way with me.

When I came back to earth, I looked over at them. Laz had sat back on their heels, a wicked glint in their eyes as they licked my arousal off of their lips.

"You are beautiful when you fall apart, Athena," Laz whispered to me, causing my heart to race.

"Are you satisfied, baby girl?" Silas asked, slightly less breathy than he had been just moments before. I wonder if he found his release. I wished I could have watched it.

"Yes, Sir." I smiled, closing my thighs slowly, not missing how Laz watched my every move with hungry intent. I almost leaned forward, ready to give everything and more to this person on their knees before me. Laz stood, grabbing my legs and throwing them open. I bit down on my lip again when they pulled me to the edge of the bed. I felt their hard cock notch at my entrance. Their eyes watched mine eagerly as they pressed forward slowly.

"Blood." My whole body froze as Silas said the word. I pulled back from Laz, and my arms crossed my body, covering what I could as I turned my head to look at the screen. Laz did as well, a look of equal confusion on their face. I saw Silas' face, and it was shock that colored his expression. As if he couldn't believe he said the word either.

"Sorry.. I uh." He was floundering. Laz turned to the camera so I couldn't see their face. Silas ran his hands down his face. "Fuck. Sorry. I just…" He leaned forward, closer to the screen so I could see the flecks of color in his irises. "The first time I see you speared on a cock baby girl, it's gonna be mine." My breath caught in my throat and Laz turned back to look at me briefly.

I slid off the bed and threw my robe back over my body as Laz gathered their clothes too, dragging their pants back up and fastening them. I took the moment to study them, now that my head wasn't clouded with lust. They had that kind of strength that wasn't obvious. Without a shirt, I could see the definition of muscles. They were one of those sneaky buff people. Their abs were there but had softer edges, much like the person to whom they belonged. Everything about Laz told me they were a chivalrous person, the one who will be kind to you, and care for you. The epitome of southern hospitality. But everything I just experienced told me that they held the capacity to destroy everything in their path. Myself included if I let them. And I just might.

"You were perfect, Athena. I'm sorry. I'm not used to sharing…yet." Silas said, tossing the last word to Laz who looked at the screen. The edge of dominance was gone from his tone,

"You did a great job of it." I smiled at him, feeling on cloud nine. Not only had I just had the first orgasm that didn't come from my toy in years, but I let someone else watch. I'd never even been eaten out before, let alone let someone else watch me as I come undone on someone's tongue. But in this perfect, sated afterglow I couldn't bring myself to feel embarrassed.

"Thank you, both of you," I said, tossing looks at both of them. Laz crossed the floor to me, pulling me into a hug. Gentle, soft, sweet. I sunk into it.

"I was the one who had the utter privilege of tasting you today, it's I who should be thanking you." I blushed into their chest. "I should probably head back, we just got ourselves a rental." My heart flipped.

"You're staying for the season?" I asked a little too eagerly, but I just had a taste of desire with them and I didn't want to stop. Well, they were the ones who had the taste but you get it.

"Looks like you're stuck with us," Silas added from the phone. I smiled like an idiot then, because I was happy. Because for the first time in a long time, I felt like I had autonomy again. I felt like I was allowed to want something and I wanted them.

I grabbed my phone and walked Laz to the front door. They gave me a sweet kiss, not long enough to send me into another frenzy, but long enough for me to taste myself on their lips and moan into their mouth.

When I finally let myself close the door and say goodbye, I leaned back against the doorframe and smiled, looking down at the handsome man on my screen.

"Well that was something," I said, an incredulous giggle escaping my mouth. He laughed with me, much more carefree now that we were out of the game. I liked that I got to experience both sides of him.

"You were something I never expected, Athena." I noticed that my nickname 'baby girl' was no longer in his vocabulary. Maybe that was just for the game, just like 'Sir'. I smiled. I liked our game. I wanted to play again. Soon.

"I can confidently say the same." He sighed.

"Can I see you tomorrow?" He asked as if I would say no.

"I work until eight, but then I'm free," I replied, twisting a strand of hair between my fingers like a girl in love. Fuck, I needed to get a grip. They were only here for the season. I couldn't fall for them.

"I'll see you soon," he promised, and I believed him.

After hanging up, I took a long shower, letting myself reflect on the last hour of my life and how utterly unbelievable it all was. Davia would never believe me, but I needed someone to talk to about it or I was gonna lose it.

ATHENA: Davia, are you sitting down? Buckled in? Strapped down? Don't answer that. But boy, do I have a story for you.

DAVIA: Not strapped down. And probably won't be for a while. Greg's been at the police station all day. Louis hasn't come back yet.

I furrowed my brow, reading the text again. Where would Louis go after attempting to rape someone and getting caught?

ATHENA: Maybe he went home?

DAVIA: That's what I said, but Greg hasn't heard from him. Police aren't being much help though. Something about not being gone long enough yet.

ATHENA: That's weird.

DAVIA: You didn't see him go anywhere? Didn't hear him talk about going to see someone or anything?

I swallowed the lump in my throat. A sort of fear prickling at the edges of my senses. The story I told Davia was not the real one. She didn't know the sexy strangers had pulled him off of me and 'sent him on his way.' Was that all they did?

ATHENA: No. I have no idea where he would have gone.

DAVIA: Oh well, ok. Anyway… Your story.

She responded again quickly, before I had a chance to.

DAVIA: You fucked them didn't you?

My jaw nearly fell to the ground.

ATHENA: What?! How did you… No, not exactly. But it's better.

DAVIA: How can it be better than that?

DAVIA: Which one was it?

ATHENA: That's the fun part.

DAVIA: The chick? She was definitely your type.

ATHENA: They're all my type.

I answered honestly. Because it was the damn truth. Each and every one of them was a gorgeous fucking specimen. They each appealed to a different part of me. Laz made me feel safe. Silas made me feel desired. Samara made me feel powerful. And Orpheus… he made me feel seen.

DAVIA: Fair point. So which one?

ATHENA: The one with the tattoos…

DAVIA: Get it, babe!

ATHENA: And the shorter one…

DAVIA: …

I waited for a moment for her to respond.

DAVIA: Shut the fuck up.

DAVIA: You did not have a threesome.

ATHENA: Not exactly.

DAVIA: Details babe, details.

I spilled the whole encounter over the next several texts, each scandalous deed had my body igniting with the memory.

DAVIA: …

DAVIA: ….

DAVIA: How fucking dare you live my dream?!

I laughed, I could practically hear her saying this in my head.

ATHENA: It was the hottest thing I've ever done.

DAVIA: And you didn't even have sex?!

ATHENA: I didn't need to.

That was kind of a lie. I definitely needed it, like primally. But I understood why crossing that line in that scenario wasn't the best idea. I wanted each of them, but I think I wanted them alone first.

DAVIA: I'm so jelly it's not even funny.

ATHENA: Says the woman who is used to having wild sex nearly every night of the season with handsome strangers.

DAVIA: You're right. I'm so lucky.

I rolled my eyes, laughing as I typed my response.

ATHENA: You have to promise not to let me get attached.

I crawled onto my bed, wrapped in my towel, and pulled my knees to my chest.

DAVIA: Babe, the fact that you think you even have the potential to get attached is why I won't promise you a damn thing. You have no idea how hard it was seeing you close yourself off from everything, and everyone for so long.

Davia saw me at my worst. She and my mother were the only ones who truly believed me when I told them what happened to me. She saw every gritty detail, each horrid scar, physical and otherwise. When I was trudging through hell trying to find my way back to the light, she was right beside me, holding my hand.

ATHENA: What if I fall apart when they leave?

DAVIA: Then that means you were healed enough to break.

DAVIA: There was a time we weren't sure that would ever happen.

Tears began to fall down my cheek as I read the words. Was it possible that I had healed from that night? The road seemed so dark, so treacherous that at times I truly never thought I'd be able to see the light of day again. But that's the thing about healing from trauma, it isn't fast, it isn't even gradual, it's torturous, slow, and grueling. It takes years of enduring darkness until you see the light. But when the sun finally shines on you again? It's fucking worth it.

ATHENA: I love you.

DAVIA: I love you more.

DAVIA: Have a great wet dream! <3 talk tomorrow.

I chuckled and tossed my phone on the bedspread and swapped my towel for a baggy t-shirt. My whole body felt electrified like tonight was some sort of dream. I was giddy, and excited. Already planning my outfit for tomorrow. I hope he wasn't too attached to me in dresses because I was out of them and I didn't have the money to go out and buy a new one every time I saw them.

I slid under the covers and curled up with my phone in my hand, smiling as I scrolled back through my messages with Silas.

Before I thought better, I composed a message.

ATHENA: Goodnight, Silas. Thank you.

I was about to lock the phone and set it aside for the night when his response came in.

SILAS: Goodnight, Athena. If I could dream, I'd dream of you.

It was a strange thing to say, but it still had my heart in absolute flutters. I was in a lot of trouble.

It was with new memories of my body being worshiped that I fell asleep, and for the first night in a while, I didn't dream of *him*.

ARCHER

FOURTEEN

My fingers were stained with blue paint, already drying and cracking with each movement as I packed up my truck. I tossed a glance at the wall in front of me that was cast in the warm light from my headlights.

The symbol was easy enough to draw, even without any artistic abilities. I was a musician, not a painter. Well no, I guess I wasn't a musician either anymore. I'm a Hunter.

Right.

Keep forgetting that part.

We received intel the day before that a vampire was spotted in this town. I say we, but it's the head office that gets the calls and distributes the jobs. In the last three months since my father's not-so-gentle reminder that it was time for me to join the ranks, I've been sent to just about every state, and about a hundred towns to plaster this symbol on every surface. I'm a fucking messenger at best. But I guess, if I had to be dragged into my dad's business, this was a good way to do it. Not like I particularly want to go around staking vampires. So yeah, I guess being the resident artist wasn't too bad of a deal.

Although I had only recently joined the team, I'd grown up knowing the truth about the world we live in. It's so much scarier hearing stories of the monster under the bed and knowing that they're real. My dad made sure of it. *"You need to understand that you are only ever safe in this world if you fight for your safety."* He would tell me that, daily. Pretty sure it was cross-stitched on a pillow in our house somewhere. I didn't resent my father. In fact, I was thankful that he devoted his life to protecting me and other humans from the monsters that lurk in the shadows. I guess, I just never thought I'd have to do that too.

My phone buzzed, and I instantly felt my shoulders tense. Where were they sending me next? Somewhere warm I hoped, although that wasn't common. I'm learning quickly that these creatures like to stay away from heat and sun. Probably because their disgusting flesh would rot off if they were in the sun for too long.

I relaxed when I realized it was my personal phone, not the work one, that was ringing. But it didn't last long when I saw the name of who was calling. I answered on the fourth ring. "Bennett." Don't let me fool you, I'm not the cool guy that answers the phone by saying his last name for any other reason than I saw it on Criminal Minds once and thought it was awesome.

"You finished with New Hampshire?" I offered a glance over my shoulder at the wall with the fresh blue paint.

"Yeah, just packing up." I slid into the front seat of the truck and turned the key in the ignition.

"Good." I waited for a moment for him to continue.

"So what am I vandalizing next? A billboard in Montana? A bakery wall in New York?" I heard him sigh on the other end of the line.

"It's time for you to start pulling your weight, kid." My brows furrowed as I pulled away from my latest art project.

"Those paint cans are pretty heavy," I retorted, knowing that wasn't what he meant.

"You've put off your initiation for too long." I gripped the steering wheel tighter, my foot pressing into the gas pedal a little too hard. "I can't keep covering for you."

"I know, dad." He'd been as understanding as he could be, I got that. If I was going to be a part of this business, part of the Hunters - even if I didn't want to - I was going to have to prove myself.

"Listen, there's been talk around the office. They don't like the way you've been dragging your feet." His voice quieted. "People who drag their feet can be pulled in the wrong direction. They think you might be a loose end." I swallowed hard, letting up on the gas, watching the speedometer return to a legal limit. "Do you know why Nameless doesn't have any traitors?" I nodded although I knew he couldn't see me. But he knew that I did. I'd heard him say that a million times. "Because they don't let people live long enough to betray them." Fuck. My father whispered one last thing, his voice was threateningly low. "Your resistance is going to get one of us killed. Maybe both."

My father was a good man, as far as I knew. He fought to protect the human race, how much more of a hero can he be? If my lack of motivation for the family business was going to be a threat to his life, I needed to get my shit together.

"Ok, what do I do?" I begged.

"They're not making a move on you yet, but they're watching. You need to do something big, and soon." I turned into the parking lot for my motel, parked, and flipped off the car, but I didn't move, just sat there staring at the brick wall ahead of me and listening to my father speak. "You need to find The Wanderers." I ran my hand through my box-dyed black hair with blue tips.

The Wanderers were our white fucking whale. The only vampires to ever escape our clutches after being brought to our headquarters. I was a teenager when it happened, but I remember hearing about it. It's all anyone could talk about. And when I finally started my service at Nameless, it was the cautionary tale we were all told. They escaped after taking down fifteen of our best recruits. It took years for them to rebuild, to get their strength back. From what I've heard, they've been chasing them since that very day, with no luck. The Wanderers consisted of five of the world's strongest vampires, well four now. Luckily, Nameless managed to pick off one while the others got away, weakening their numbers and probably effectively pissing them off. My father has told me the stories of how he was the one to land the killing blow on the former fifth member. Driving the wooden stake directly into her dead, cold heart. He earned himself a pretty big promotion that day. The Wanderers were each gifted with a supernatural ability, something we'd only just begun to test when they escaped so to this day, we don't understand it entirely. But we knew enough to know that they were damn near untouchable.

"How the hell am I supposed to do that?" I pleaded with him. He had to know that I wasn't cut out for this job. I could barely make it through training, let alone catch the most elusive and powerful coven out there.

"I have intel on where they might be. A source of mine from outside the network." My father never told me he had a contact on the outside who knew about Nameless and the existence of the things that go bump in the night.

"Who is it?" I asked eagerly, knowing that he would never tell me but deciding to ask anyway.

"No one you need to concern yourself with." A cryptic answer. Typical. And pretty par for the course with my old man.

"So this outside source was able to track The Wanderers before Nameless?" How was that possible?

"Don't worry about it."

"You're not giving me many answers here," I sighed.

"Stop asking questions you know damn well I can't answer." My father was a strong man, built like a fucking brick house. His entire torso was covered in battle scars, gunshot wounds, knife wounds, and bite marks. I traced a featherlight touch across the raised scar on my wrist, a reminder of who I should trust, and who I shouldn't.

Vampires cannot turn a human with a simple bite. Thank god for that, otherwise, most of the Hunters would be part of the legion of the undead by now. No, it was a lot more complicated than that. Had something to do with a shared transfusion or something? I don't know, I wasn't really paying attention to the training that day, I was mostly trying not to pass out. Blood made me a little queasy. I paid attention just enough to know I shouldn't drink a vampire's blood. Done. Got it. Say no more.

"Where are they?" I asked timidly, knowing very well that my father was about to send me into the lion's den and I was just a little gazelle. No, you know what. I wish I were the gazelle, but I'm that stupid kid that fell into the enclosure. At least the gazelle was part of the natural food chain. Not me, I'm just the idiot who got too close.

"My contact spotted them near some town called Shockgrove. Maine." I leaned back in my seat, stretching my legs. I glanced longingly up at the motel room I had booked for the night, knowing full well that I wasn't going to be sleeping there any time soon. Maine wasn't that far, I could be there by morning.

"Got it."

"I do not need to remind you how important this is. For both of us." He didn't. I knew. I fiddled with the rearview mirror, sliding it so that I could see the backseat and the duffel bags of supplies. The paint cans and the paint brushes were in the bed of the truck, where it didn't matter if people saw them. But these bags, full of the standard issue weapons any Hunter has the good sense to never leave the house without, those stay hidden. As much as I didn't feel like I belonged in Nameless, I was pretty handy with a wooden stake, not that I've actually staked a live vampire yet. Just the dummies we use in training. But still. I could hold my own. I've been sculpting my body to be a perfect weapon for most of my life, just like my father wanted me to. Guess it was time to finally use it.

"I won't let you down, dad." I wasn't sure if it was the truth, but as I put the car in reverse and headed back down the highway toward Maine, I knew I would do anything in my power to make sure it was.

SAMARA

FIFTEEN

Coffee didn't have the same effect on vampires that it did on humans. It took effect quickly but burned out quicker. I took slow languid sips, willing the magic concoction to take away this vicious headache I woke up with.

"You looked stupid happy last night," I offered to Laz as they sauntered into the kitchen of our rental. They had gotten home pretty late, and when they did, gone was their hostile attitude and reckless anger toward Silas. Replaced with something cheerier. And it didn't take a vampire to smell the lust on him. And not just any lust. Hers.

I hated how I already knew the intimate scent of Athena's arousal, but I did. I knew it and it made me feel wild.

"Or just stupid," Orpheus called from the back patio. He had the doors thrown open and was staring down the beach, watching. I knew what he was watching for. And I prayed we never saw it again, but I understood that was too big a wish to come true. Not while the Hunters were alive. Not while Nameless still existed.

Soon enough I would stop running and eradicate their stupid existence. I would not leave this life without dragging every single one of those fuckers with me to the grave. I'm undead, I belong in hell. So do they.

Laz ran a hand down their face, groaning. And I shook off my bloody revenge-filled goals to truly look at their face.

Their eyes were red-rimmed and bloodshot. Their skin was paler than it had been last night and their fangs were slightly elongated.

"Are you hungry?" I exclaimed and Orpheus was to us in a moment, his eyes scanning Laz's face.

"Fuck. You've got to be kidding me." Orpheus slammed his fist down on the granite countertop, it groaned under the pressure but didn't break. Thank god, because it's literally day one and I don't want to lose our security deposit already.

"What's going on?" I asked, looking between Laz and Orpheus.

"Those two, love-sick puppies, are hungry already." I furrowed my brows.

"What does that mean?" I hadn't heard of this before. A vampire getting hungry so soon after feeding? We'd just fed two nights ago. But even as I considered the improbability, a pang groaned in the pit of my stomach. Hunger.

Orpheus bounded up the stairs with reckless abandon, I quickly followed behind taking the steps two at a time. Laz didn't follow. I wondered just how weak they might be feeling. Orpheus threw open the door to Silas' room, and as I approached from behind, I gasped as I looked past him.

Silas sat on the ground, his back up against the bed but he had a hand on his stomach as if holding himself together. His cheeks were slightly sunken and his eyes were vacant of his normal cocky glow.

"Fuck, Silas. You ok?" Orpheus was down on his knees beside him in a moment while I stood in the doorway in shock.

"I'm just fucking hungry," Silas groaned. I sighed, thankful that he was alive, and seemingly still just as much of a jerk as always.

"How is this possible?" I asked anxiously, glancing between Silas and Orpheus as they exchanged a silent conversation.

"I don't know," Orpheus offered.

Once the shock wore off, I slid in on Silas' other side placing a hand on his cheek, and then I felt him. Sending my vibration of power through his body, my mind settling into his skin and dancing amongst his poisonous blood searching within him for the source of this ailment.

In life, I was an empathetic person. I think that's why I developed this gift when I was ushered into my second life. Despite the lot in life I was handed, and the terrible existence I had, I still tried to understand. Tried to see everything from their point of view, and put myself in their shoes. It was second nature. That's what got me through it all. The evenings at that disgusting building with horrid men claiming my flesh as if it was something they had been owed. I convinced myself that they did it because they needed to and that they wouldn't do it if they had another choice. Although, eventually I stopped trying to understand why my parents did what they did or why men were paying for my unwilling company. Stopped making excuses for them. At some point, you have to realize that bad people are just bad people no matter whose shoes you're in.

Silas' blood felt normal, I couldn't find any physical issues with his body. In fact, infuriatingly, he was in tip-top physical shape. But there it was. A void, hunger. It was palpable, I felt it in my own stomach as I discovered it in him. My fangs elongated slightly to accommodate the new hunger growing.

I pulled my hands back, severing the contact, and I felt the hunger subside slightly. I was feeling some mild version of the pain he was in. "What did you feel?" Orpheus asked. He was good at masking his emotions, probably from years of feeling others so strongly, but at that moment I didn't need his gift to see the worry painted on his face.

"There's nothing physically wrong with him," I started. "He's just…hungry." Silas lifted his hands in an exasperated motion.

"See, I told you so!"

"What does this mean, Orpheus?" A thought solidified for me. What if that man we killed was toxic? Laz was a little preoccupied that night, so they didn't check the quality of that asshole before we kinda dug in. Panic started to set in, if we had drunk soiled blood would this happen to all of us? Was it already starting for me?

"It means we have to leave," Orpheus spoke clearly. Confidently.

"No," Silas and Laz, who had finally made their way up the stairs, spoke at the same time.

Orpheus groaned and stood, pacing about the room.

"You need to feed, and we can't do that here!" Orpheus was right. It was a small enough town that any disappearances right now would be suspicious. We were lucky that the douche from the bar hadn't hit the news yet. But it would. They always did in towns like these.

"We will be careful." Silas tried to stand, finding his arms weak and eventually leaning back against the bed frame defeated.

"You can't even stand up, Silas!" Orpheus was losing it. Frankly, I understood that. This was unprecedented, and none of us knew how to proceed.

We hadn't even reached this level of hunger when the Nameless held us, not until the second month without blood, at least. But here they were now. Starving.

Why?

"I'm not leaving her!" Silas growled, his eyes bearing as much intensity as he could muster.

"I agree," Laz added from the doorway, where they had found a solid spot to lean against.

"Don't you two think this is some kind of fucking omen or something? You need to forget about this human and let us get out of here." Orpheus was nearly begging. I'd never seen him so out of sorts before.

"Don't you think it's rather interesting timing? We meet her, and all of a sudden we're hungry like we are starving for her! If you're looking for evidence that she's our mate, then there it is," Laz spat out. Tension filled the air. Orpheus' eyes burned into Laz and they stood their ground as tall as they could.

Wait, did they say "our" mate?

"You already scented her." Orpheus was grasping at straws, desperate to protect our family. He always has been. And I could see where he was coming from here. I was just as afraid of Nameless catching up to us again as he was. I knew the things they could do to us just as well as he did.

But if she truly is their mate, they deserve the chance to find out.

He knew that too, or else he would have bought this house for us. He was giving them the chance they needed, but he was worried too. Hell, the two of them just fed two days ago and were acting like they may desiccate within the hour. I'm worried for my family too.

If she belonged to both of them, maybe there was a chance she belonged to someone else too. I shook off the budding hope blossoming in my chest, forcing myself to picture Alora's gorgeous features instead of the sweet redhead down the road.

"You need to scent her blood soon," I spoke up. Three pairs of eyes found me. I stood and walked toward the window, shrouded in a dark grey curtain that kept the sun's rays from reaching my skin.

"What if it's not clear yet?" Silas asked, quietly. A simmering anger boiled within me as I thought about what he was referring to. Her blood that night had felt impossibly inhuman, toxic to nearly the point of no return. There wasn't a doubt in my mind that she would have died had she drank even a sip or two more. I don't understand how someone could do that. I also don't understand why it made me so angry, made my dead heart feel like it was constricting inside my chest.

It might be hypocritical of me to condemn a human for being a monster when that is exactly what I am. The difference is, I am the monster that people know to watch out for, not to invite in, the one from the stories meant to scare little children into submission. I'm a monster because I'm meant to be. Humans are monsters because they choose to be. Humans are subtle. You don't suspect them. You don't distrust them. But I've lived a long time, and there are humans who are more monstrous than I could ever be. They just blend in better.

"What if when she bleeds our hunger takes over?" Laz asked, quietly in a whisper.

"We won't let you hurt her," I said, immediately. It was the truth. I wouldn't let Athena be in harm's way. Not again. Even if I had to stand up against my family to make it so. Which was a strange thought that sent an even stranger emotion coursing through me.

Orpheus glanced my way, and I tried to shake the feeling he had surely felt within me.

"But just to be safe, you should feed before you see her." If for no other reason than to return their features to a more… normal look. Athena might not know what a hungry vampire looks like, but anyone with eyes could see that these two weren't at their best with their dark red-rimmed eyes and hollowed cheeks.

"We cannot hunt here," Orpheus reminded us.

"Then you and I double back," I said to our leader. "We head back the way we came a few hours, lead the trail in the wrong direction, and bring back a snack." I tried to calm the excitement I felt at the prospect of feeding. My hunger was growing every second. Orpheus looked like he didn't want to consider it, but to his credit, he didn't dismiss the notion immediately.

"It's a good idea, Orpheus." I leveled my stare at him, watching as he took his bottom lip between his teeth, holding in the retort he had prepared. Releasing a sigh and lowering his head, he nodded.

"Fine. Samara, let's go." Silas and Laz looked hopeful, a smile spreading across their faces. "You two, stay here and don't do anything stupid until we get back."

"Ah, but we can do something stupid when you return?" Silas joked and Orpheus leveled him with an annoyed glare before stalking out of the room. "Be back by seven, I have a date!" Silas sighed, relaxing again. Laz stepped aside to allow Orpheus to leave past them and then slowly moved into the room, sitting on the bed above Silas.

The two of them shared a knowing glance that held a deeper meaning than I had the ability to understand. Something like respect or acceptance passed between them. How had they gone from nearly ripping each other's arms off, to this? I wondered briefly if Silas could scent Athena's arousal on Laz as clearly as I could, and if so, why was he so calm about it?

"Do you think it's true?" I asked them both. "That she's yours?"

They exchanged another glance and Silas faced me once again, looking so feeble from his position on the floor. "I know it with every fiber of my being, with every phantom beat of my dead heart. She is mine." He looked at Laz. "She is ours."

My breath caught in my throat. "Ours," I repeated. So they intended to share the human? Why?

And why was I suddenly very envious of that notion?

"Then we will make sure you are well enough to see her tonight. To know for sure." I left the room and went to the room I had claimed for myself down the hall. It had pale blue walls and sandy shag carpet. The white lines on the bed were only slightly ruffled from my body weight on top of it the night before. I switched my sundress out for some comfortable dark black leggings and a black, off-the-shoulder sweatshirt that was perfect for going hunting. Blood didn't show up on black.

When I met Orpheus on the ground floor, he had swapped his suit for dark black pants and a tight black t-shirt. He looked disheveled, a far cry from the leader of The Wanderers Coven that I had come to know. This human was throwing everything off balance.

Love often did.

He led me to the rental car he had somehow gotten a hold of and we climbed inside. He must not have wanted to run, this time. The interior was a dark leather that felt hot against my cold skin as I settled down into the seat. Orpheus was quiet as he pulled down the driveway.

Silent questions hung in the air. But I knew he wasn't ready to ask or answer them so we sat in the quiet for an hour as he drove us back the way we came.

Shockgrove was a town that was so small, so insignificant, and yet it was changing everything.

Athena was changing everything. I just hoped we could survive it.

ORPHEUS

SIXTEEN

I'd never been the type of person to fall apart.

In fact, in my life, those that fell apart were often ripped to pieces. In order to survive this world we were in, you needed a cool head. I had that. I prided myself on being the calm one - the lighthouse in a storm. You do not survive as long as I have, with Hunters around every goddamn corner, without critical thinking, without planning. You don't survive as a coven in this world without understanding what it takes to survive, and doing it.

Something is happening to me here in this fucking town. For the second time in my long second life, I'm feeling shaken, and unstable. The first time that happened was at the hands of Nameless. I can't help the eerie feeling in the pit of my stomach telling me that I am so close to falling victim like I did last time.

I made the mistake of getting comfortable once, and we lost Alora because of it. I refused to make the same mistake again.

Yet, here we are, our coven in disarray, breaking every rule we've ever made. Rules that have kept us alive, kept us safe. All for a fucking human.

She's got a pretty face, sure. But no one is worth ruining my family for. No one.

"What are you going to do if it's true?" Samara asked, quietly from the passenger side. We would drive most of the way, just back to where we last stopped before making the unfortunate mistake of walking into a bar at Shockgrove, then getting out to run. Leaving our scent, and leading whoever is watching in the wrong direction.

Then we'd hunt.

I pondered her words for only a moment. "It's not," I answered her. She clicked her tongue, I saw her shake her head in the corner of my eye. "It's not," I said again, although it did sound less convincing the second time.

"Ok." She didn't sound too convinced herself. Her hands were folded in her lap as she watched me. "But what if it is?"

What if?

A mate was sacred to our kind. And rare. Not rare in the fact that they don't exist, but rare because of how our kind was Hunted so brutally, we seldom lived long enough to find the one to whom our soul belongs.

If Silas and Laz found their mate in this fragile human, I could only see three ways this story could play out.

First, Nameless would find out, because somehow they always did, and kidnap her. They'd use her to lure The Wanderers to their headquarters and when they had us in their grasp, they'd torture and kill her while we watched. Then they'd kill us, the way they tried to all those years ago.

Or she will die, either from an accident or illness or in old age, as humans are inclined to do and her death would cause catastrophic, irreparable damage to our coven.

Or lastly, and arguably the most improbable of the options, they would mate, she would agree to be turned and we'd add another vampire to our coven.

Even if that were to happen, we'd still be hunted. We'd still be vulnerable. More people in the coven meant more people that Nameless could use against us.

No, there was no happy ending here. There couldn't be.

"What we've always done," I said as I pulled off the highway into a rest stop. We'd run from here. Samara got out of the car, watching me with careful eyes. "Try to survive it."

The next hour was nothing but quiet breaths and the rustling of the ground and twigs beneath our feet. It was spring, so that meant that life was starting to begin again. It was an interesting concept. Rebirth. How something could die, and stay dead for a long while only to be born again. Find a way back to life.

An interesting concept, but ultimately impossible for someone like me.

Not that I'd ever wanted to be human again. I've been what I am for centuries at this point. The tiny shack I once called home in Romania is a distant memory at this point. Blurred by time and the way human memories seemed to dissipate the further we were removed from them. I don't recall the majority of my human life anymore. Nor do I care to. I like the person I am today. The monster I've become.

I love the family I've built, and I would do anything for them. Including this stupid, reckless hunt.

Samara and I made it to the city by midday, being sure to stay in the shadows of buildings and beneath awnings as much as we could as we stalked silently through the alleyways. We never hunted during the day. We weren't interested in having witnesses. But also, the type of person we hunted normally came out at night. For some reason, evil felt more comfortable in the moonlight.

We'd made the decision long ago, that if we were going to kill, it would be those who deserved it. Like that asshole from the bar. I felt my jaw tighten with anger every time I pictured his body pressed up against hers. Like he owned it - like he deserved her. I relished ripping his throat out, but now I wished I had made it last. I should have taken my time. Made him suffer.

He was a monster, I was his karma.

Samara and I wordlessly made our way through the metropolitan streets. Being not as careful as normal to cover our tracks. We wanted Nameless to track us here after all. We had drifted to the seedier part of town, where the bars didn't have windows and the cars had busted windows. In our experience, in the many years of hunting, we've found that those who live in areas like this aren't the monsters, but those that often found places like this comfortable, so they took advantage of it.

I couldn't stand people who took advantage of anything or anyone.

Samara nodded to a small white brick building, sounds of general debauchery and mirth flowed from the door. We entered together, making our way across the sticky wooden floor to the bar. Neon signs illuminated the space. Five or six patrons sat in chairs scattered about the bar, and a few scantily dressed women walked around with trays in their hands, as some danced atop the tables while the men ogled them.

Samara and I took two barstools and glanced around. Listening. We'd find our next target here, I was sure of it. The stench told me as much.

The bartender was this buff guy with tattoos that rivaled Silas'. He wore a jean button-down shirt, with the sleeves ripped off, exposing his tanned skin and the myriad of black and white pictures painting him. He had a deep scar that ran from above his eyebrow to his cheek and it gave him that sort of 'don't fuck with me' vibe that I could appreciate. He approached and set down a napkin in front of the two of us.

"Girlie, you're in the wrong place. The male dancers ain't here till Thursday." I rolled my eyes, contemplating if bigotry was enough of a reason to choose this guy for our hunt.

"I ain't here for the boys, buddy," Samara responded leaning onto the bar. The bartender looked at her all perplexed for a moment before his face scrunched up in confusion.

"You don't look like one of those girls who likes pussy," he scoffed, flinging the towel in his hand over one shoulder. I gripped the wooden bar top to keep from reaching across the space and bashing his head in.

"And you don't look like an asshole so… wait, actually I guess you do." I managed to hold in my chuckle, but barely. The bartender looked angry, his gruff face turning slightly red.

"You gonna tell me you're a faggot too?" He said as he looked my way. "Get on out of here. We don't want your kind in here." And that does it. I glanced at Samara who looked back as if to confirm what I already knew. We had found our mark.

The bar was crowded, so we needed to isolate him. This is where Samara came in handy. I just hope that he'd fall for it, as everyone else had. By the time she turned back to face the bartender, her mask was firmly in place and she was the sensual bait she knew how to be so well. She leaned on the bar, pressing her arms together to push her breasts out just enough to be enticing for him. I'd never found Samara attractive in that way, despite it being obvious she is a beautiful woman. I guess, when I first saw her, I couldn't see anything but the broken girl, the girl whose parents had taken every ounce of light from her and snuffed it out. She was beautiful, sure. But it was her heart and her soul that called to me that night and every night for the following month. Not her body.

The bartender, like a typical 'alpha' male, looked down to appreciate the view she was offering down the neck of her loose-fitting sweatshirt.

"I said I wasn't here for boys," she whispered, seductively. "I'm here for the men." I had to force myself not to roll my eyes. I was disappointed, but not surprised when the bartender leaned forward into her space with a cocky smile on his face as he fell for her charms. Hook, line, and sinker.

For being such 'strong' and 'powerful' men, they always were the easiest to kill. It's almost like the whole 'alpha male' bullshit was exactly that…bullshit.

"Well, little lady, why didn't you just say that." He licked his lips and I nearly gagged. How Samara was able to keep a straight face as these men acted like fools in front of her was beyond me.

"I gotta take a leak," I said nonchalantly, slipping off the stool and heading back to the bathrooms. I knew Samara was watching, so she knew where to lead him when it was time. I watched the patrons as I walked, too engrossed in the show in front of them to realize we had even come in.

I hid inside the girl's restroom, in one of the two stalls. With any luck, the dancers had their own dressing room, and wouldn't be coming in here any time soon. We just needed enough to fill the flasks we each had stashed away in our pockets. It was going to be too risky to take more than that in daylight. But this should be enough.

Although, what we drank two nights ago should have been enough too.

While I waited for Samara to convince the asshole to join her in one of these disgusting stalls, I let my mind wander. Athena couldn't be their mate. She was bleeding that night, and the bond should have solidified had it been there. But I guess if I'm looking at the facts a little closer when we saw her in that position and saw what he was prepared to do to her, Silas and Laz definitely went off the rails a bit. So did I, for that matter. Which I didn't really understand. Why did we care so much, why were we blinded by our anger at that moment? I'd never lost control before. I'd never broken my own rules before. But there I was, changing everything. For her.

Infuriating, stupid human.

She was going to get us all killed. There were rules for a reason, they were supposed to keep us safe, and keep us from making mistakes and falling into Nameless's grasp again. It took so much from us the first time. Our security, our friend. I don't think we'd survive it if we had to do it again.

A few minutes later two bodies came spilling into the bathroom. I heard Samara's fake laughter as she pulled him into the room. Her hands went to his collar turning him so that he was facing away from the stalls.

"Damn girl, you just made my day," he said in a pathetic attempt to sound sexy. I rolled my neck back, stretching out. Letting the monster that hides beneath the surface of my nearly impenetrable skin come out to play. I felt the shift happen, like an old friend returning after a long trip away. Samara giggled unconvincingly, but he wouldn't care. He was the type who'd never care.

I quietly pressed the door open, the slight squeak of the door drowned out by Samara's fake moans of anticipation. His large body was leaning over her as she sat on the sink. His mouth was on her neck, sucking away. How ironic. Her eyes met mine and I nodded, moving closer. Always stalking my prey.

I was inches from him when I caught my reflection in the mirror behind Samara. My dark hair which was usually slicked back into place, was wild, hanging haphazardly across my forehead. My pale skin looked almost grey, with the tint of death. But the most captivating part of me was the full set of pointed teeth. The canine teeth on both the top and bottom rows were the longest, begging for this man's blood. My irises were bright red, and crimson veins nearly blocked out the whites, making it look as if a pool of blood was looking back at me. My ears had a slight point to them now, a feature we got from our bat ancestors. At my side, I flexed my hand feeling my nails elongate to a dangerous point. I was horrifying. The type of monster you'd see in your nightmares. The kind of monster that you could never be safe from. The type of monster you'd only see once. The face of evil itself.

The bartender's unsuspecting eyes flick up to Samara, glancing only briefly at the mirror before the horror settles on his face. He looked back to Samara only to find that she had shifted too. He was sandwiched between two demons. With nowhere to go.

Do you think he knew he was looking at his death?

Before he could scream, my fangs sunk into the skin of his neck. Silencing him. His call was drowned out by the rush of blood that was filling his mouth.

Blood.

It tasted like life. Like a promise. I swallowed greedily until I knew the man in our arms was dead.

"The flasks, Orpheus," Samara reminded me, her eyes fixed on the dripping red liquid as it traveled down his throat. I barely pulled myself back. There was a hunger within me that I hadn't realized was there before. Had I begun to fall prey to whatever hunger was plaguing the others? And if so, why?

Samara and I held the waste of space up and drained the remaining blood from his pathetic body into the flasks. Filling five of them before we ran out of space.

"There's still some left, Samara," I said, wiping the corner of my mouth. "Drink up."

She did. Sinking her fangs into his neck and drinking what little blood we left in his veins. Once she was done, she licked the wound, and the violent-looking punctures closed up, leaving smooth skin where our fangs had pierced him. I watched my reflection in the mirror waiting for my features to revert. My fangs receded, giving way to the white set of teeth beneath. My eyes returned to their dark shade, the red fading into nothingness. The tips of my ears rounded and I felt the elongated fingernails return to their normal length. Soon enough, the Orpheus that I presented to the world was the one looking back at me. The one who women often fawned over. The one who seemed trustworthy, handsome, and alive.

But I was the same monster I always was, no matter which face I wore.

ATHENA

SEVENTEEN

I sighed deeply as I watched the clock on the wall. It was nearly closing time and we had three customers all day. The Maine Plotline was holding on by a thread. And so was I.

I started counting the drawer early, luckily I had my date with Silas to look forward to. I still couldn't believe what had happened last night. That kind of thing doesn't happen to girls like me. That happens to Davia, but never to me.

Except, it did happen to me. My body still tingled with the effects of a phantom orgasm. While I still had a lot of questions about what happened, why and what I should do next…one thing was abundantly clear. I wanted to do it again. I smiled at the vase of roses that sat on the counter. In a way, they were perfect to represent my strangers. They were soft and sweet like Laz, their pink shade was subtle and beautiful like Samara, but their scent was strong and intoxicating like Silas' presence. And then there were the thorns. Orpheus. They will leave eventually, just like these flowers will die. But with any luck, their presence here will bring me as much joy as these flowers have before it's all over.

The bell above the door rang, clueing me into the arrival of a customer. I eagerly made my way around the counter to greet them. Greg rushed in, looking around with a sort of frantic wide-eyed gaze. My heart rate picked up, half expecting to see his predator friend trailing him. I sighed deeply when I realized that he was alone.

He rushed forward, his dark skin looked ashen and his features were haggard. That clued me into the reason for his visit. Louis still hadn't turned up.

"Hi, Greg, right?" I asked as he reached me. His eyes scanned me furiously.

"Where is he?" He asked, a little unhinged and breathless. I took a step back, carefully placing the counter between the two of us.

"If you're talking about Louis, I haven't seen him since he left the bar." Greg ran his hands along his scalp.

"He never came back," he whined.

"Maybe he went -" I started.

"He did not go home!" Greg slammed a fist on the counter. I took another step back, a bit of fear gripping my heart.

"Ok, I'm sorry. I don't know where he went. We left the bar, went our separate ways and I haven't seen him since." I spouted the tale that I told Davia, knowing she would have relayed that to him.

He shook his head, looking down at the counter, his fists balling on the surface. I watched them with caution. I ran down a list of my escape routes, something you learned to do after going through what I did. I could head out the back, but he would be able to catch me. I could run for the office where my Grandma was currently doing intake inventory. But then she's in danger too. My eyes are scanning the area for anything that might be useful if it were to come to that.

"What did he say to you?" He was desperate, the bags under his eyes told me that he hadn't been sleeping since his friend left.

Disappeared?

I thought back to the anger pouring off Silas, Laz, Samara, and Oprheus when they told me what happened to me. They wouldn't do anything to him, would they?

"He asked to buy me a drink, I said no," I told him, truthfully. "Then I wasn't feeling well so I left." That again was true. But here's where the truth became fuzzy. "He walked me out, but I said goodnight and left, alone," I spoke slowly, carefully. Without the ire, I wanted to invoke. Just thinking about the fucking waste of space made my blood boil, but I wasn't going to do anyone any good if I told the truth now.

He pushed off the counter, spinning away from me with a strangled grunt. He was angry. Worried. I get it. If it was Davia, I'd be out of my mind with worry.

"I'm sorry, have you tried calling him?" I asked, but immediately wished I hadn't because he turned his eyes to me with such hatred that I felt it in my chest.

"Of course, I've tried fucking calling him." I took one more step back.

"I'm sorry," I whispered, trying to placate him. He groaned and put his hands into the pocket of his navy blue pullover hoodie.

"If you can think of anything else, please just call me. Davia has my number." And with that, he was gone and I felt able to breathe again.

I could have told Greg that the strangers from the bar were witnesses. But they didn't know the lie that I told Davia. I started to panic when I thought about the inconsistencies I was already creating. If - heaven-forbid- there really was something going on, and the police got involved, I was not going to look good. I needed to tell Silas and the others not to tell anyone. But then I felt guilty immediately about asking them to lie for me, even though I knew they would. Which was strange, because I don't even know them, but I feel like I know their souls. As corny as that sounds.

If Louis was missing, maybe my strangers knew something about it. Maybe they could help find him. Although, the idea of finding him was not appealing in any way, shape, or form.

I mulled over that thought for the next half hour as I cleaned up the front of the shop. The bell sounded again and I felt fear grasp at me for only a second before I turned and confirmed that Greg had not returned. Or worse, Louis. The man standing in the doorway was tall and slender, with more subtle muscle definition. He was facing away from me but I noticed his paint-covered pants and hands. An artist then? I smiled as I took in his dark black hair with electric blue tips poking out from beneath his baseball cap. He turned to look my way and his hazel eyes searched the area before landing on me.

"Hello! Welcome to The Maine Plotline," I cheerily offered, giving him a bright smile. He wore a white t-shirt, which wasn't much lighter than his pale skin. Dark freckles dotted the canvas of his body. "Can I help you find anything?" I didn't add the 'please', but it was there in my tone.

"Just looking around," he said, stiffly, although his eyes were warm and welcoming.

Feeling his gaze on me had me wishing there were other sets of eyes watching me right now. Laz, Silas… Samara…Orpheus.

I shook my head, simultaneously ashamed at how I let my mind wander to such dirty depths, and shocked because I met someone out in public, and instead of immediately being wary and nervous, with my mind reverting to its protective hole, I was thinking about the future, the possibilities. Maybe Davia was right, I was healing.

"Actually, do you have any records here?" I nodded, smiling. Bringing music to the store was one of the things I implemented when I officially took over. Grandma fought back against it, saying that we had our niche already and shouldn't mess with it. But since the success of the first shipment, she's been pretty quiet about it. In this day and age, you have to keep up in order to stay in business. Our little town didn't have a music store, so I filled that hole as best I could. Niche or not, we needed to adapt to survive. Next step…social media. Groan.

I led the man down the aisles, through the stacks toward the back wall. I'd decorated it with posters of some of my favorite bands growing up and I had a little corner nook set up with a cheap record player for someone to sit and enjoy.

"Here you go!" I fanned my arm out, showing off my contribution to The

Maine Plotline's character. "There's not a huge collection, but we've got some good stuff in there. A few rare finds." He stepped forward, flipping through the selection.

"Are you looking for anything in particular? We've got a pretty nice amount of recent records, but I've got to admit I'm a bigger fan of the 70s and 80s."

"They certainly don't make music like that anymore, do they?" He spoke under his breath, pulling out a copy of Led Zeppelin's Self Titled album and scanning its condition.

"I agree!" I added eagerly. He tossed a smile my way before returning his attention to the record in his hands. "Led Zeppelin, good choice."

"You know, my favorite story about this band is how they got their name," he said, pointing to the album in his hand. "Entwistle was recording with Page, Paul Jones, and Beck when they were tossing around the idea of starting a band so he said-"

"That their band was going to go over like a lead balloon," I finished for him. His eyes met mine and a friendly smile spread across his face sending warmth to my chest. It was a safe smile, a promising smile. I liked it. I wanted to see it again.

"Yeah, that's right." He slid the album back into its place, his fingers quickly flipping through the rest. He took a breath, turning toward me with an excited look in his eye. "Ok, you can go to a concert for any singer alive or dead, who are you picking?"

I leaned on the wall, crossing my arms across my chest and thinking for a moment. Pondering his question, and enjoying being able to talk about this kind of stuff with someone.

"Freddie Mercury," I answered finally, earning an appreciative 'oooh' from the stranger. "Videos aren't enough, that's a performance you need to see live."

"You're completely right about that," he smiled.

"What about you?" He flipped through the bin, stopping when he came across a vinyl of Born in the U.S.A. "Springsteen, hands down."

"That surprises me." I mused.

"He's one of the best performers in the world," he argued, playfully.

"I'm not disagreeing with you!" I said, throwing my hands up in mock surrender, laughing with him. "You just don't seem like the Springsteen type."

"Oh yeah? What type do I seem like?" I took a step forward until I was on the other side of the bin of records, flipping through until I found London Calling by The Clash. I pulled it out and handed it to him.

"This seems like you."

"In what way?" He asked, scanning the album in his hands.

"Purely going off vibes." He chuckled at that.

"Well, I'm glad my vibes have good taste." He held my eye contact for a few long seconds before looking down again to continue his search through the records.

"In town for the season?" I asked, for some reason not wanting the conversation with the new customer to end. His hands ran along the front of a Chicago album.

"What?" He asked, turning his head toward me again as if he didn't hear what I said.

"The season, are you here for the tourist season?" Why was I so nervous? Why did I suddenly wish I could be friends with him? Why did I suddenly feel like I was yelling?

"Ah, no. Just passing through," I nodded, feeling a twinge of disappointment. I liked talking about music with people. Davia didn't understand it all that well, and Grandma hadn't listened to any new music since 1979.

"Well then, thank you for choosing to spend some of your short time here with me." I felt my face get hot. "With the store, I mean. Not me. Like you're not with me. You're here for the books and records. And maybe some coffee too? I have that. We have that." I chuckled awkwardly, wishing the ground would open up and swallow me whole. I desperately didn't want him to think I was flirting with him. I have enough hot people to warm my bed. The stranger's eyes softened and he smiled at me, his boyish, stubble-covered face lighting up.

"What's your name?" He leaned forward over the collection of records, resting his elbows on the wooden frame of the display.

"Athena."

"Nice to meet you, Athena." He shook my hand quickly, without a hint of lust or attraction, just a friendly encounter. I didn't feel leering looks being tossed my way or unwanted advances. I appreciated that almost as much as I appreciated the music discussion. He stood straighter, returning his gaze to the music.

"Well, I'll leave you alone, let me know if you need me," I paused, my eyes widening. "Anything. If you need anything." He smiled, a laugh bubbling in his chest and I turned away fighting the urge to facepalm.

When I arrived back at the front desk, I felt a giddy excitement fill me. Despite the many terrible things I've been through in my existence, I was still living. I was letting new relationships come to me, being open to embracing them. This stranger isn't sticking around, but instead of cowering away from him, I made conversation. I made a friend, for however brief a time it was. That's something I never knew I'd be able to do again.

A few minutes later, the stranger made his way up to the front, an album in his hand. The Clash, London Calling. I smiled at it as he slid it on the counter over to me.

"Great choice," I mused, ringing him up, trying to contain the bubbly satisfaction building in my chest.

"Yeah, I dunno, it just feels like the right vibe," he joked, fishing his wallet out of his jean pockets. I once again noticed the cracked paint on his skin.

"It's The Clash, of course, they have good vibes." He grinned, sliding his money across the counter.

I went to grab it, the tips of my fingers brushing his hand briefly, our eyes met quickly before I glanced away, clearing my throat and finishing the transaction.

"Are you an artist?" I asked him in an attempt to dissuade his burning gaze.

"I'm sorry?" He reached for the bag as I handed it over the counter to him.

"You have paint on your hands, are you a painter?" He looked down at his hands, his bag hanging from one finger. A strange expression crossed his face as he surveyed the blue paint that was dotting his skin.

"Ah, no, just helping someone paint something." He said, closed off, stuffing his hands into his pockets. The playful banter between us was gone. I nodded, quietly, suddenly confused about the entire interaction. The stranger didn't say anything else as he headed for the door.

"Wait, um, you never told me your name." He stopped with a hand on the door handle and looked over at me. His hazel eyes were filled with secrets I'd never know.

He looked as if he was waging a war within himself, but ultimately he smiled softly and said, "Archer."

He was gone before I could respond, and I filed away the interaction under people I'd never see again but would think about from time to time. How could I not with his kind face, his knowing eyes, and then there was the mystery.

"You go ahead and take off girlie, let me close up tonight." The sweet voice of my Grandma shook me from my fantasies. I turned to see her, standing behind me. She was older, and her body had begun the slow rebellion that everyone had to deal with as they grew up, but she still had a lot of life in her. She was the type of Grandma who fell in love with the 70s. Her hairstyle and clothing still reflected that. Her lower half was covered in bell bottoms and her yellow, white, and red vertical-striped shirt had bell sleeves that dangled off her wrists as she walked. Her kind green eyes were just like mine, and mom's, but her red hair had long since turned white.

"I can do it, Grandma, don't worry! You should head home and rest. Do you need me to walk you home?" She waved her hand as if to say I was being ridiculous.

"I'm an old woman, not an invalid. I can close up the shop tonight." She hip-checked me out of the way and took my spot at the counter. I chuckled.

"Are you sure?" I asked eagerly. The excitement for my date was quickly overshadowing my worry about the store. Which sent a burst of guilt directly to my heart.

"I've been closing this shop since long before you were even a little swimmer in your dad." I made a gagging sound.

"Stop, I beg you." She laughed and took a seat on the stool, separating the cash for counting. She hardly ever mentioned my dad. I knew they knew each other from the brief time that he and mom were dating, but he up and left 'the minute responsibility started weighing on him'. Grandma's words. I didn't ask her anything about him, all I know are the tidbits that the two of them used to slip into conversation. I don't care to know him. I watched her work for a moment. Her hands were wrinkled, her body frail and skinny and she paused to remember her place more than a few times. Something like fear coursed through me. I didn't want to lose her. I couldn't lose her.

But I would. And probably sooner than I would like to.

"Get out of here will ya? You're making me lose my spot." She waved me off and with a lackluster chuckle, I left.

It was bittersweet, having her here. On one hand, this bookstore was her baby. She built it from the ground up with my Grandpa, and it was her dedication that kept it alive. On the other hand, now when she was here, she was here alone.

When she lost her husband, my Grandpa, her world was shattered. She still had us, sure, but there's something so heartbreaking about losing your soulmate. She was a strong woman, and she's been moving on as best she could, but I could tell that there was a certain light in her eyes that wasn't as vibrant anymore.

"You've created something really special here, Grandma. I don't think I tell you that enough." She turned to me, leaving the cash on the counter in piles. Something like happiness swam in her expression.

"We all did. Every single person who's stood behind that counter has brought something important into this store." She was walking toward the bookshelves now, counting cash long forgotten.

Her hands came up and ran along the wooden shelves. "Your grandfather built these with his own two hands. After we spent our life's savings on this building, we didn't have two nickels to rub together." I had heard the story a million times, but I never tired of it. "He took a job at the lumber yard down the road just so he could get some of the discarded lumber for free." She traced her fingers along one of the very 'imperfections' she was referring to. A knotted piece of wood, which at one time had made that log unusable, but now it was what made the character. It was history. "That was his contribution. He built this place." She smiled, sadly. She loved talking about him, but it hurt her too. It always would.

"I was in charge of getting all the books you know, for the grand opening. Now, ask me how I got those books without a penny to spend on them. Go on, ask me." Her eyes shined with a bit of pride.

"How'd you do it?" I asked, sliding my backside onto the counter to sit.

"I drove to just about every library and bookstore on the East coast and convinced them to give me their overstock. They normally donated it or sent it back, but yours truly got them to give it to us. We opened the store with the strangest mod-podge of books you ever did see, but it worked." She laughed, and it was a melodic sound, it reminded me of my mom.

"You brought the music." I didn't miss the almost indignation in her voice at that. "And your mother brought the heart." She said softly.

"Yeah, she was good at that," I added. Grandma wiped a tear from her face and made her way back to the counter.

"Now, you need to go out there and make a baby so we have someone to take over when you kick the bucket." I choked on air and struggled to catch my breath, laughing along with her. It was a hollow sound though, seeing as I wasn't sure we'd survive the next year, let alone another generation.

"Gee, thanks, Grandma." She shooed me off the counter and started sorting through the piles again.

"Get out of here so I can count this dang cash, alright?" I leaned in, planting a kiss on her cheek, and then headed back to the office to pick up my purse. Walking through the stacks at The Maine Plotline felt like taking a trip down memory lane. No matter how much time has passed since the ones we love left us, their memory was as strong as the scent of freshly brewed coffee in the morning. Always here with us, embracing us. If I was ever missing mom or grandpa too much, I'd take a walk through the aisles to feel them again.

Leaving the shop, and stepping out into the cool Maine air, I found myself smiling. The pier was gorgeous when it was empty. Despite the financial and economical issues that came with a quiet town, I loved seeing it in this state. Quiet. Serene. Peaceful. The sky was a soft orange-pink as the sun neared the horizon, casting a brilliant light on the shimmering surface of the water. Seagulls dotted the sky, filling the air with their call. It was peaceful. Calm. It was home.

I felt the hairs on the back of my neck stand on end, not in fear, but in anticipation. There were eyes on me. I could feel them. It was a possessive glance. Eyes that felt like they knew me. And I wanted them to watch me forever.

I turned my head, seeing the culprit leaning against one of the light posts, his arms folded across his broad chest. He wore a tight black shirt with a white jean jacket. His muscular thighs nearly burst through the black skinny jeans he wore and a bouquet of pink roses was clutched in his hands. I found myself sauntering over to him before I had the good sense to stop myself. I worried only briefly about reacting this way to someone I only just met. What if I scare him away? Before I could worry, Silas stood up to greet me, rushing forward and throwing his arms around my waist. I clasped my hands around his neck and suddenly my feet were lifted from the ground as he held me. I laughed into his neck, the sound was carefree, hopeful. I'd missed feeling this free.

"Hello to you, bookworm," he chuckled against my hair, tightening his hold on me. Suddenly a thought occurred to me, Silas had been calling me bookworm, but when we were…well doing what we were doing last night, I was 'baby girl'.

Like he had a different nickname for the 'me' in the bedroom.

I liked it. I felt like I had some kind of sexual secret identity, like a sexy Batman.

Silas set me down on the ground, my feet feeling secure but as he loosened his hold on my body, I somehow felt more off balance. Strange. I smiled up at him, his eyes searing into mine with an intensity that I'd come to expect from this man before me. I couldn't help the blush that spread across my face as I thought about our phone call last night, my skin felt blazing hot.

His fingers came up to trace featherlight touches across my cheek. He looked at me with such reverence, like he was in awe of what he was seeing, the way someone might look at a work of art or a wonder of the world. I'd never been given such attention before. It felt unearned but warm and welcoming.

"I love the way you blush." If I was flushed before, now I was a tomato. He chuckled, as his ice-cold knuckles graced my skin. He offered me the roses, and I smiled brightly and gripped them. "For you."

"You spoil me," I offered as I took a deep inhale of the delicious scent.

"We're just getting started." He winked and I had to press my thighs together to stave off the aching need building.

"Let me drop these off inside," I said, turning to head back to the shop. When I entered through the front door, the bell rang making my Grandma look up from her counting.

"Welcome to the - Oh, Athena! What are you doing back already? Was he a two-pump chump?" I choked on air and devolved into a coughing fit.

"Grandma, Jesus…" She laughed and I stepped forward, carefully adding the new bouquet to the vase with the last one. I smiled like a fool at the very full vase.

"Your grandfather used to bring me roses too," she mused, quietly. Smiling weakly at the arrangement. "The good ones always bring roses." I smiled, my cheeks already burning from the amount of happiness Silas had brought me.

"I'll see you later, Grandma." She gave me a wink and I was back out the door and standing in front of Mr. Tall, Dark, and Sinful himself.

"Come with me," he said, weaving his icy hand with mine and leading me down the pier toward the parking lot.

"Where are we going?" He simply tossed a coy smile over his shoulder and continued to the lot. He led me to the passenger side of a dark pickup truck. I tossed a quizzical look his way.

"You don't seem like the pickup truck kind." He laughed as he settled in the driver's seat and took off down the road.

"It's a rental." I nodded. We drove for a few moments in comfortable silence and I let my head drift to face him. He was relaxed in his seat, controlling the wheel with only his left index finger and thumb, his elbow resting easily on the door. His right hand, however, was in my lap, gripping my hand. I found myself trying to memorize the feeling of his hand in mine as if it was too good to be true. A dream that I really wanted to remember when I finally woke up and returned to the life that I deserved to have. The boring one, devoid of the type of passion that the man sitting next to me elicited. Holding his hand in mine felt like grabbing a handful of snow in the middle of winter, his frosty skin biting into mine. How was he always so cold? I might have written it off as a medical condition, had Laz not felt the very same. I tried not to dwell on that peculiar fact, but I couldn't help it. I studied him. The planes of his face were sculpted as if from marble, he was nearly perfect. His handsome, chiseled face was smooth, unblemished, and taunting.

"Like what you see, bookworm?" Silas joked, peeking over at me coyly from the corner of his eyes.

"I'm staring, sorry." I turned my head, diverting my eyes to look at his hand. My fingers danced along his skin, exploring him.

"I don't mind," he whispered with a seductive lilt to his voice. I smiled to myself but didn't meet his eyes again.

"Your hands are always so cold," I spoke, almost to myself, but I knew he heard me because his hand tensed slightly in my lap. I silently prayed I hadn't hit a nerve.

"Yeah, sorry about that," he said, nonchalantly, but I could sense his hesitation. He made no move to pull his hand from mine, but his grip loosened and I didn't care for how that created a pit in my stomach.

"It feels nice," I said, truthfully. Every time I was around him, and Laz too for that matter… and who was kidding Samara and Orpheus too… I felt like I was burning from the inside out. Like any moment my entire body might burst into flames that consume me in heated passion. So having their cool touch to balance me out felt…perfect.

"Good to know." He chuckled, using his thumb to rub circles on the soft spot of my hand near my thumb. I smiled like an idiot while I watched the movement. So simple, and yet it said so much.

A thought occurred to me then, the image of Greg's disheveled appearance, his threatening aura. I shivered.

"What's on your mind?" Silas asked.

"Oh, um, Greg visited me at work today. Louis's friend. The uh-" I paused, taking a deep breath. "The guy from the bar." Silas' hand tensed and I swear I heard a growl rumbling in his chest.

"Did he do something to you?" He asked through clenched teeth.

"No. He's just, well Louis hasn't been seen since that night and he's getting really worried. He was asking me questions," I said meekly.

"Do you want me to get him off your back? You don't need to talk to that douchebag's friend." I squeezed his hand appreciatively.

"It's ok. I um, ok this is going to sound bad, but I didn't tell Davia about what happened with Louis." Silas was quiet, waiting for me to continue. "She was happy with Greg, and she's already had to help me through too much in my life, I didn't want to burden her with yet another traumatic Athena story." We came to a stop at a stoplight, it cast a strange dark hue in the car. Silas looked threatening in the red light, but I wasn't afraid, if anything I felt safe. Like he would protect me from anything.

"First of all, you are not a burden, nor are the things you've survived." His eyes bore into mine. "Second, you don't owe your truth to anyone, not even your best friend if you don't want to give it to her." I sighed, not realizing how much guilt I'd been harboring over the whole thing.

"If he's actually missing, the police might get involved, and if that's so, Davia and Greg are going to tell them my story. The one I've been telling them. That we left the bar and went our separate ways." I didn't want to ask him to lie for me, especially if the authorities got involved. I felt sick to my stomach.

"As far as I'm concerned, that's exactly what happened," he said clearly, watching me with his honey eyes. The light turned green and he continued down the road. I felt a weight lift off of my chest and I held his hand tighter.

"Thank you," I whispered, looking ahead at the road. We drove in silence for a few minutes, but my curiosity, or fear maybe, got the better of me.

"Did you see where he went, after… After you got him off of me?" I asked, timidly. I wasn't sure I wanted the answer.

Silas looked like he was thinking, a soft smirk on his lips. "I think he headed West, saw him walking toward the gas station down the road from the bar." He looked like he had said something humorous, and I couldn't help but furrow my brow.

"Ok, I'll text that to Davia to tell him. He'll like to have a lead." I sent the message quickly, then returned my phone to my bag. Deciding to put the whole situation away. I was on a date and I was going to enjoy it without the ghost of Louis screwing it up.

I glanced up as I felt Silas turn off the road. It was starting to get darker, the sun creeping toward the horizon. His headlights lit up the sign for the Field of Films drive-in-theatre. I'd been here what felt like a million times growing up, my heart leaped in my chest. For a brief second, it wasn't Silas next to me in the car, but my mom as we drove in for yet another night of stuffing our faces with junk food and making fun of the characters on screen.

"Wait, Silas. This place isn't open for the season yet." I tried not to sound disappointed as we drove down the annex road toward the very empty field. Normally, this road is packed, bumper to bumper with cars of families coming to spend the evening under the stars.

"The owner needed to do a test run of the screens and projectors before the big season opener, and he was more than willing to let the owner of The Maine Plotline be the guinea pig." I smiled, Charles Greene owned the drive-in and he and I would often find ourselves in light-hearted arguments about films versus their book sources. He was yet another friendship I let fall to the wayside after everything happened. I should fix that. The pergola that sat at the end of the road at the entrance to the field was lit by soft white fairy lights and the string of Edison bulbed lights hung across the whole field strung from post to post, dotting the sky above the field with a soft starry glow. It was gorgeous, one of my favorite places in the world. I hadn't been back since before Mom passed. It never really felt the same. But driving toward the screen now, with Silas, I wasn't dreading it. I was thrilled. Despite my final memories here.

Silas slowed down by the pergola, where Charles was standing with a large smile painted on his face. "Charles, thanks again for hooking us up!" Silas spoke to him as if they were old friends, not strangers. And by the laugh that Charles gave him, he felt the same camaraderie.

"Thank you for agreeing to be my practice. I always hated doing the test run." Charles leaned toward the car window and his eyes landed on me. "If it isn't Miss Landry. It's nice to see you." He didn't say it with any modicum of judgment for my absence which felt nicer than I thought it would.

I leaned toward the window, trying hard not to focus on how being closer to Silas made me literally erupt in goosebumps, and smiled. "Hi, Charles! It's really nice to see you too." He nodded, his eyes holding a small ounce of pity. He knew my mother and probably missed her as I did.

"So what are we watching?" I asked, leaning back and removing myself from Silas' immediate aura because he was entirely too alluring and Charles was the one who was supposed to be putting on the show, not the other way around.

"Double feature tonight consists of Jumanji and Zathura," Charles said with a false presentation as if he was practicing for his future customers to return. "Pull forward, no matter where you park, you've got the best seat in the house." He laughed at his own joke and I couldn't help but smile at him.

Charles turned to the table behind him and grabbed a tub of popcorn, a large drink, and a box of Twizzlers, handing them through the window to Silas who took them and sat them on his lap. "There's the snacks you ordered! The station is 97.4. Well, enjoy the show. I'll be back to switch the film!" Charles disappeared into the projector building and Silas drove forward.

"You've been here for two days and you're already getting special favors from the locals?" I joked while taking a sip of the drink he had bought us. His eyes lit up with mischief as he turned to me.

"You offering a special favor, bookworm?" I choked on the drink and very unflatteringly had to cough to regain composure. He chuckled and parked, facing us the wrong way.

"Uh, I hate to be that guy…but the screen's that way." I pointed over my shoulder, but Silas was already getting out of the truck and walking around to the bed. I turned in the seat, looking through the back window of the cab.

Silas fiddled with a chest that had been strapped down in the back, opening it and removing items. When I finally got out of the truck and made my way to where he was working. I saw the several blankets and pillows he was pulling from the chest. Once he'd gotten his materials out, he placed the chest on the ground and got to work laying out the plush blankets into the truck bed. In a few minutes, the back of the truck looked like a cozy little hideaway.

"You came prepared." Silas slipped off his shoes, letting them sit on the ground before climbing up onto the bed and offering a hand to me. I did the same, letting him pull me into the back.

"You don't think I'd just drive a truck for fun do you?" We smiled at each other for a moment, a sort of romantic tension washing over us as we stood in the back of his rental truck with the soft twinkling lights shining above our heads from the string lights and the stars.

His eyes burned into mine, our breath mingling with each other. I didn't want to move, to break this spell because it felt unreal, like something out of a fantasy. He must have felt the same because he didn't move for a while, he just stood there, holding me in his arms, looking for forever in my eyes.

His lips brushed against mine and I sunk into them. Letting him taste me the way I so desperately wanted to taste him.

It was a fairly chaste kiss, probably because we both realized at the same time that the projection of the screen had started up, and Charles could no doubt see us standing up in the back of this truck. Silas pulled back with a grin on his face and slid down onto the blankets. He reached through the small window of the truck to the radio and set it on the right channel before settling down onto the pillows and blankets. He looked up at me, patting his chest and inviting me to snuggle into him.

I did.

That's how we sat for quite some time, while the previews played and I heard Charles' car drive off, leaving us alone. The movie began, and I watched with distracted attention. I couldn't focus on Alan Parrish and the shoe factory with the solid wall of muscle beneath me. My hand rested on his chest and I would get brave enough every so often to trace the planes of his stomach through his shirt. I heard his breathing catch, but he didn't react any other way.

"This is a perfect date," I whispered, instantly embarrassed. "I love this place." I tried to cover.

"Did you come here often growing up?" Silas asked, his lips resting against the top of my head.

"Mom would bring me all the time," I admitted, quietly.

"And now?"

I sighed, taking a breath. "She's not around anymore, so I haven't been in a few years." It was easier to admit this to him since I couldn't feel his eyes on me.

"Loss fucking sucks. I'm sorry you have to deal with it." I nodded, gripping his shirt and fighting back tears. It would be just my luck to cry on my first date with one of the hottest guys in the entire world.

"Thank you." I held back the waterworks, despite the stinging eyes. "Have you lost many people?" I asked because his tone had a sort of melancholic pain to it.

"Nearly everyone," he admitted quietly. My heart shattered. This strong-willed person next to me was harboring so much pain behind his playful eyes and it sent a vicious sting directly to my chest.

"Silas, I'm so sorry." I felt him shaking his head.

"I got used to it. Doesn't mean it sucked any less, but I'm not surprised when it happens anymore." His fingers ran through my hair softly as he spoke. "I'm numb to it now. The pain."

"Being numb doesn't mean you don't feel pain, it means you've experienced too much." He sighed.

"I guess you're right."

"Although, maybe it would be nice to feel numb about it. It's been a few years and I'm still feeling so raw, exposed." I traced my fingers along his abdomen mindlessly.

"Is it hard having so many places in town that hold memories of her?" He spoke softly, comfortingly. His hand was stroking my back.

"It was. But now I think I'm lucky that I feel her all over this town. That way I won't forget her." I hadn't said that out loud. That I was worried about forgetting her. When you lose someone… you lose them twice. Once when they first leave you, and again when you start to forget. When you can't recall the exact smell of their presence, when you drive past a place you used to go together without thinking about them, when you hear a song and can't hear their voice singing along. The second loss isn't talked about enough, but it's just as painful.

"Tell me about it?" He asked, quietly.

"About what?" I asked.

"About when she would bring you here." He wasn't pushing, but it felt like an honest invitation to share some of my favorite memories.

"We had this old hatchback, so we'd sit in the front seat together with all the widows up. We were so squished." I chuckled, the image of the two of us cramped inside the car, with blankets and pillows like we had created ourselves a little fort. "She would save up all month so we could splurge on all the drinks and popcorn we could eat." I smiled into his chest, a warm feeling spreading within me despite the coldness of his body against mine. "Sometimes, we would turn off the radio and we'd play a game and try to guess what the actors were saying on the screen."

It was a chilly summer night with the misty air rolling in off the ocean. Mom and I were packed into the hatchback with all our snacks. The flickering screen ahead of us was some romantic comedy. We had been laughing all night, my stomach hurt and probably partly from the excessive amounts of candy I had consumed.

"Ok, let's play," Mom said, turning the volume all the way down in the car and thrusting us into silence. "I'll take the older woman."

I smiled, situating myself in the car so I could fully see the screen, ready to play our game. The younger character came storming through the front door and the parent tried to stop her. My Mom spoke up, a thick southern accent coming from her mouth. "Now you listen here young lady, where have you been?" I giggled, chewing on a milk dud as I responded in an equally over-the-top accent, I think it was supposed to be Australian but ended up vaguely Eastern European.

"I'm a teenager now, Mom, I don't need to tell you where I am all the time. Jeez."

The Mom on-screen chased after the daughter and grabbed her arm. "You can't run away from me, girl. I told you I had something I needed to tell you tonight." Mom continued.

The teenage character went to slam the door, "Leave me alone! I'm brooding!" Mom and I both laughed, watching the action on the screen.

"It's important, and you're not gonna like it," Mom said as the character on screen pushed into the teenagers' room and paced along the floor.

"Unless you're here to tell me that we can get pizza tonight for dinner, then I don't care!" I said, playing the part.

"I have cancer," Mom said, I chuckled a little watching the character on screen scream something at her kid, Mom's character confession didn't fit the scene.

"That was pretty bleak mom, jeez," I said in my own voice before picking up with the character, trying to match the indifferent look on her face. "You're totally killing my vibe." I retorted in the accent, waiting for Mom to respond. The parent character began to speak, but Mom didn't. After a few seconds, I turned to glance at her. She wasn't watching the screen anymore. Instead, she was watching me. Her eyes glistened with unshed tears.

"Mom?"

"I'm sorry, baby. I didn't know how to tell you." A tear slid down her cheek and she wiped it away quickly. Breathing became difficult and my entire chest felt tight like I might fall to pieces at any moment.

"No," I said simply. Shaking my head. "No, that can't be. You can't be…" She reached out, grabbing my hand and pulling it into her lap.

"I'm so sorry." She watched me as if I was going to break, which I very nearly did. Shattering into pieces in the front seat of her hatchback.

"We'll fight it, we'll get your treatment. We'll fix this…" I couldn't fathom losing her. She was everything I had.

"It's not that simple, sweetie." She went on to describe to me her diagnosis, and the very bleak prognosis.

I learned two things that night.

One, my mother had cancer.

And two, that cancer was going to take her and there was nothing we could do about it.

I didn't realize I had tears streaming down my cheek until I tasted the slightly salty liquid on my lips.

"She sounds wonderful. I wish I could have met her," Silas' voice rumbled in his chest. It was saddened, comforting.

Then he moved from beneath me, sliding me off so he could reach into the truck through the window. I sat up, trying to wipe the remaining tears from my cheeks before he saw.

A few moments later, Robin Williams's voice was silenced and Silas was sitting back down. He looked at me, then spoke in an atrocious Russian accent. "I am going to play this game and there's nothing you can do to stop me." A laugh escaped my lips, nearly causing me to snort embarrassingly.

"What are you doing?" I whispered, despite us being entirely alone in this field.

"I believe it's your line." He gestured to the screen where Bonnie Hunt was mouthing something. I nodded, exhaling a quick laugh of disbelief.

"Who said anything about trying to stop you, I just want you to keep me out of it." Silas devolved into a fit of laughter at my positively horrendous English accent.

"At least let me borrow your dice, you know yours work better than mine," He continued, his accent even thicker and more incorrect.

"You can't blame the dice when you're the one who's bad at the game." I had tears pricking my eyes again, but this time from joy.

"What accent was that supposed to be?" He asked through breathless laughter.

"It was better than yours!" I retorted quickly, finding myself smiling deeply, freely. Silas watched me for a moment, his laughter slowly receding but leaving his smile firmly in place. Then his lips were on mine, claiming me as his own. I tangled my fingers in his long dark hair, pulling it from its tie at the back of his head until it fell loosely around his face. I drew him closer to me, rising onto my knees to get closer to him. He held my body flush against his. His hands firmly pressed against my back and ran along my spine in a taunting dance. My tongue pressed against his and he greedily kissed me.

My hands gripped the collar of his jean jacket, sliding it down his arms until his biceps were exposed and my fingers gripped at them, loving the way they strained as he fought to get closer to me.

His wicked fingers grabbed at the hem of my dress and tugged it up, but not removing it. I silently thanked him. We were still outside, and despite the very dirty things I planned on doing with him right now, I didn't want to be that exposed.

His hand teased the skin of my thighs and I felt my core tighten in anticipation.

With a hand firmly on the small of my back and one nearly touching where I needed him to most, he leaned me back onto the bed of the truck. The blankets cushioned me. His mouth went to my neck then, his lips hungrily kissing me there, I heard his groan with frustration as if he couldn't get enough of me. I knew the feeling. I lifted my hips to meet his. I felt his erection just beneath his jeans and right then, right there, I wanted nothing more than for him to devour me.

SILAS

EIGHTEEN

The scent of her arousal was driving me into a near frenzy. I had to force myself to refrain from sinking my fangs into the perfect flesh of her neck and discovering once and for all if she was my mate. Although, at this point, I didn't care. There was no way I was leaving this girl, not now, not ever. Mate or not.

My hands danced closer to her core and she moaned into my mouth, pressing her hips up. Seeking me. I ripped through her panties, literally ripping them apart like some sort of feral beast. She gasped into my mouth and I swallowed it.

I kissed down her neck again, ignoring the temptation to take her throat between my teeth and drink, and traveled down her body until my head sat nestled between her thighs. She moaned, arching off the bed of the truck and I smiled as I took her in. The camera phone didn't do her any justice. I didn't waste a second before dipping my tongue into her heat. The taste of her exploded in my mouth, flavors that I never knew were possible. It was a breathtaking, habit-forming kind of taste. A type of straining desire that I'd only ever dreamed of. She cried out as I feasted on her. Taking her clit between my lips and sucking, following her body's cues. When she pulled my head toward her center, I slid my tongue into her core as far as I could reach, letting her control me like she controlled that toy last night. She'd never need it again. Not while I was around. Her breathing became shallow and I felt her thighs shake with promised euphoria. I thrust two fingers into her and she exploded around them. I lapped up her release like I was starving for her. I'd never need anything else again. Not after having her.

"Baby girl, I need to feel you," I spoke with a strained jaw, crawling up her body and using one hand to free myself from the confines of my jeans. If I didn't get inside of her soon, I wasn't going to be able to refrain from tasting her the way I needed to.

"Do you have a…" She paused, her eyes landing on my cock. I gently pressed it against her clit, letting it slide in her arousal along the surface of her cunt. Never pushing in.

"I.." I paused, sliding along her opening. I didn't want to drop this bomb at this moment, but it was important for her to know. Especially because I never intended to have a barrier between me and her. "I can't have children, and I haven't been with anybody in a long time." Her eyes flicked up to meet mine, and her flushed skin looked radiant. Gorgeous, like the goddess she was. But a sort of sadness was in her gaze.

"I'm sorry to hear that," she breathed quietly.

"Don't feel sorry for me, I'm about to fuck the most beautiful woman in the world. I'm the luckiest guy alive or dead." She smiled at that, but her face contorted in passion as I slid myself along her slit again, pressing down to give her just enough pressure.

She rocked her hips, begging me with her body to slam into her. But I needed to hear her say the words. I needed them since the moment she uttered them in her store, among the books. I needed her to whisper those words so achingly that I might cry out if I had to wait another moment.

"Beg me, baby girl. Beg me to fuck you," I whispered into her ear, her moan was delicious and she turned her head to meet mine. Her lips stole mine in a kiss.

She wrapped her arms around my neck and held me there as if she was afraid I'd leave. As if she was trying to meld our bodies together as one. "Don't make me ask again, baby girl."

"I need you, Silas. Fuck me…" She pulled back, her green eyes burning into mine. "Please."

I slammed into her, my cock disappearing into her heat. She cried out and threw her head back, pressing her breasts against my chest. I groaned at the overwhelming feeling of it all. She clamped down on me, her wet heat welcoming me like it knew she belonged to me and I to her. I stayed still, letting her adjust to my size, and forcing myself to breathe, to calm down from this euphoric high that threatened to cloud my senses. The feeling of being inside her was more potent and addictive than any blood I'd ever tasted. My mind was cleared of everything I'd ever known except this moment. It was only her. And it would only ever be her. Always. I'd never felt anything more perfect, and looking down at her splayed out beneath me with her legs wrapped around my hips and her mouth slightly parted, I'd never seen anything as perfect either.

Then I moved. Slowly at first, savoring the way she seemed to squeeze me with every slight movement. She met me, thrust for thrust, sending her hips up, begging me for friction. I let my fingers trail down her torso, pushing her dress to the side and finding her clit with my index finger. She gasped as I pinched it between my fingers. I watched the space where my cock was disappearing inside of her in awe. There wasn't a doubt in my mind that she was made for me.

"Open your eyes, baby girl. Eyes on me." She did and I felt that space where my heart used to reside jerk back to life as if she was a lifeline I never knew I could have. Looking at her, seeing her face as I claimed her in every way I could, I knew this woman was my salvation.

So I did what any sane man would do when realizing that he was looking at his future. I started to fuck her as hard as I could. My fingers dug into her skin, and I worried only briefly about hurting her with my strength, but she matched my thrusts with her own, taking me the way she was made to. I couldn't believe how hard it was to ration my strength when all I needed to do was rut into her and mark her as mine. My hands gripped her hips hard, guiding her down onto my cock at a speed that probably wasn't quite human, but the way she cried out and moaned in pleasure, I knew she didn't mind. See, perfect for me.

My fingers continued their torture of her clit until she was detonating around my cock, her orgasm sending her over the edge and her walls pulsed around me. I pushed through it, prolonging her blinding passion. Her fingernails dug into my back, and if I wasn't nearly indestructible, she might have drawn blood. The thought spurred me on and I drove into her, chasing my climax and once it arrived, I felt my entire world shift on its axis. I came with a type of ferocity I'd never experienced before, my entire body wracking with pleasurable jolts. I came to a resting position, my weight on her chest, listening to her heart beating wildly. Neither of us spoke for a few long quiet minutes, we just savored the sound of our breath and felt our sated skin burn against each other. I was still inside of her, and I wasn't sure I'd be able to remove myself.

I lifted myself in my arms, looking down at her. She smiled up at me, her expression one of happiness and satisfaction. I wanted to bottle it. My eyes flicked to her neck, my tongue coming out to wet my lips slightly. I felt the briefest warning that my fangs had started to elongate and I hid my face from hers by burying it in the crook of her neck. She smelled like a forest after heavy rainfall, peaceful, and calming. Her blood ran hot through her veins and I wanted to taste it. At the very least I needed to scent it so that I could confirm once and for all that Athena Landry was meant to be mine.

My mind flashed back to the promise I made before I left for this date.

"Just promise me that you will wait until we're together. To scent her." Laz had finished drinking the blood that Orpheus and Samara brought back for us and was sitting with their legs crossed looking at me.

"Why?" I asked although I understood.

"If she's ours, I want us to find that out, together," they pleaded with me.

"I want her alone first." Laz nodded, but I noticed the strain in their jaw.

"Me too."

"So we each get her alone, first. Fuck her as long and as hard as she'll let us…then we'll scent her later?" I offered.

"Please." I didn't have time to think about why I liked hearing that word from Laz now all of a sudden. Maybe last night broke some sort of wall we had built between us, but I didn't necessarily hate the idea of Athena writhing in pleasure in the middle of the two of us anymore. Not the first time though. No, I need her all alone first so I can show her exactly how wild she makes me feel.

I sighed and slowly removed myself from her, immediately feeling the loss of her around me. She grumbled something about needing to go commando now that I destroyed her panties, but I only shrugged. I didn't see the problem.

We laid back down on the blankets, her head resting on my chest and her arms holding onto me, and for the first time in a very long time. I felt my heart race.

LAZ
NINETEEN

I paced the front room, anxiously waiting for Silas to return. I tried not to picture what he was doing with Athena right now. Was he making love to her? Was he tasting her the way I had? Was he feeding on her?

No.

Silas and I may not always agree, but we're family, we're a coven and we made a promise, one I knew full well that he would not break. I trusted him. Maybe that's why I was starting to come around to the idea of sharing Athena with him.

He was an attractive guy, sure, but it was the way he looked at Athena that had me aching. The way he adoringly spoke to her, as if she was his everything. The way he commanded her pleasure. I could never give demands like that. That wasn't who I was. And it certainly seemed like Athena enjoyed that. So maybe it was a good thing she had someone else to satisfy her in an area I wasn't necessarily comfortable with. Now, I was desperate to find a place where I could satisfy her. I wanted nothing more than to be hers.

Samara was sitting on the couch in the living room, flipping through the channels aimlessly. "Sit down, will you? You're making me dizzy," she called from her seat, not looking over at me.

I sauntered over and plopped down into the cushions.

"He said he'd be back after the movies. Do you think they're…" I trailed off, not wanting to picture it.

'If I had to guess, I'd say, yes. They are." I groaned and ran my hands over my face. When I opened my eyes I saw a slight twitch of annoyance in Samara's jaw.

Samara was the first one to join Orpheus' coven. The two of them were together for a few decades before they found Silas and Alora, and then a while later…they found me.

Growing up in the south as a queer trans individual in the early 1900s before there was even a word for what I knew I was, I had never truly belonged. Uncomfortable in my own skin. Mistreated, and discriminated against for what I couldn't change. For what I didn't want to change. They didn't like that.

Samara found me one night after a particularly brutal reminder that I didn't belong because she had smelled the blood that pooled on the street beneath me. They'd left me there, intending for my mangled and beaten body to be a message to anyone else in our town who dared to be different.

Samara saved me that night. Found me on the brink of death and pulled me over, falling with me into a second life. A stronger life. Those men wanted me to be a message, a cautionary tale. Instead, I was their nightmare.

Once a human is turned, they have a brief window of time to cement the transformation, to make it permanent. The cost is death. The death of someone by your own hands. I knew immediately whose flesh would be my ticket to a new life.

Everything I'd ever known told me that vampires were evil, monstrous, death incarnate, and humans were their weak fragile prey. But how is that true if humans were the ones who damned me and a vampire was my salvation?

She introduced me to Orpheus, Alora, and Silas, and the three of them welcomed me with mostly open arms. I'm not sure Orpehus has ever been described as "welcoming" but he was thankful for the unique gift that I'd developed and suddenly I went from being forced to be something I wasn't to finally becoming *everything* I was. In every sense of the word.

Headlights shined through the window and I was out of my seat and at the door in an instant. I expected Samara to poke fun at me, to comment on my eagerness, but she was right there beside me, waiting for Silas' report of the evening.

Silas had barely set foot through the threshold by the time I bombarded him with questions.

To his credit, he answered them honestly, telling me each sweet detail of his date with Athena, without fuss. Samara even asked a few things as well.

"Did you…" I start and both Samara and I watch him expectantly. I can scent her arousal on him. He licks his lips and I wonder if he was blessed with a reminder of her on his mouth. I almost kissed him just to get a taste for myself.

"We did." He smiled to himself, a look of pure and undiluted passion and happiness on his face. I'd never seen him so content.

"Tell me," I asked, timidly. Silas and Samara shot shocked glances in my direction, but ultimately Silas found a seat and began regaling each salacious detail of the way he claimed her body. Samara perched on the arm of the couch and listened intently. I was riveted. Seeing her through his eyes. Imagining the way she writhed beneath him.

By the time he finished, I was as hot as I could be with my ice-cold skin, and I saw Samara breathing heavily at the description of Athena's soft moans. I saw a glimpse of someone sitting on the stairs.

Orpheus was propped on the top stair, his elbows leaning on his knees and he watched Silas speak with a dark heat in his red-rimmed eyes. We were all ravenous for her.

Damn.

When Silas finished his recounting of what he described as the 'single best experience he's had in either of his lives', I was out of my chair and heading out the front door.

"Where are you going?" Silas asked.

Without stopping, I tossed over my shoulder, "Where I belong."

I ran through town quickly. Taking the path that was now quite familiar to me, until I ended up at her house. The sweet blue cottage sat calmly at the end of the long drive. A single light was on the inside. I was knocking before I could stop myself. Not that I would either way.

I heard her shuffling along the floor inside the house, and I tensed in anticipation. It'd only been a day since I saw her face, but those hours felt longer than the entirety of my second life. Her mere presence was a drug to me.

The door opened and when I saw her face, I could have fallen to my knees. She was beautiful, perfect and she was smiling at me. I wanted her. I wanted all of her. I wanted everything with her.

"Laz," she said, breathlessly, but I was past the threshold and crashing my lips onto hers before she could say another word. She sank into my hold immediately, her arms resting gently on my shoulders. I kissed her with a quiet intensity, not the kind of blazing red hot passion that Silas had just finished telling me about, but the kind that started small and built and built until before you noticed it, you were at the center of a blazing inferno.

Our mouths melded perfectly, giving and taking in equal measure. My hands cradled her face, keeping her there. In this moment, with me.

I was only slightly aware of our feet moving together toward her bedroom. Nothing about our pace was rushed, or eager. It was as if time slowed and there was nothing in the outside world to worry about. There was only us, and this bond.

I pulled back from her kiss, my breathing ragged. Her room was lit by a single lamp on the end table, it emitted a soft warm glow, basking Athena's face in a soft glow that only accentuated her ethereal beauty. Framing her like the goddess she was. I exhaled sharply, absolute wonder filling me.

"You belong in the stars, Athena." She looked at me in question. "Your beauty is too captivating to view so closely. I fear you may have ruined me for everything. Museums, flowers, art. You are the most stunning thing I've ever witnessed, Darlin'. Nothing will ever compare again." Her eyes welled with tears, and her face softened with a look of adoration. I'd give my soul to have her look at me like that forever.

She reached behind her, letting her dress fall to the floor around her feet. She wore a black bra, but her lower half was entirely bare. I took my bottom lip into my mouth and bit to restrain myself from sinking down to taste her again. Not yet.

I followed suit, removing my clothes one item at a time as I felt her eyes on me. Watching me with an appreciation I never knew I had desired.

She slipped her bra off, one strap at a time, and then we were bare before each other. I felt her eyes scan me, the tension between us like a rubber band poised and ready to snap until I gave into the pull and embraced her in my arms.

So I did.

Holding her in my arms, her bare chest against mine, I finally understood what it meant to feel whole. I had been spending my entire life feeling incomplete and I didn't even realize the empty space was present until she was there to fill it. Her mouth trailed soft kisses along my throat and down my chest. Her tongue flicked against the hardened pebbles of my nipples as she explored me.

Then it was my turn. I led her gently to the bed, helping her lay back softly against the bedding. Her chest heaved with anticipation. I was taking this moment slowly. I would savor every second that I was granted the opportunity to worship her for the rest of my immortal life.

I took my time, letting my lips make contact with damn near every inch of her until she was writhing beneath me.

"Please, Laz," she begged.

"I will spend the rest of my life worshiping you, Athena. If you let me." She didn't respond other than the softest moan of approval as my tongue danced along her wet opening.

Her legs trembled around my shoulders and I pushed them apart with my hands, sinking my tongue deeper into her. She cried out.

"I need you," she whispered with seductive trepidation. I climbed up the bed until I was laying next to her. She turned her body so that she was looking at me. Her flushed face looked ever more delectable now than it had when I arrived, painted with the sweetest of blushes.

She pressed her hand on my chest, pushing me until I was on my back. She swung a leg over my hips and straddled me. I felt the heat of her center taunting my achingly hard length.

I saw a flash of something cross her face as she looked down at me. "I will use protection if you want me to, Athena. But you do not need to worry about getting pregnant with me." Her brows furrowed.

"What do you mean?"

"I can't have kids," I responded. Not exactly the sexiest conversation.

"You either?" She asked, nearly incredulous. I heard a hint of disbelief and I quickly thought of a response.

"All of us, actually. It's something the four of us have in common. We found each other because of our similar situations." Her eyes softened and I hated the half-lie I had to give her to explain why all four of us would be barren.

"I'm so sorry, that's…" She sat up, letting me follow suit beneath her, her hand gently brushing the hair from my forehead. Her green eyes held mine captive, the emotion in them was so pure I briefly worried that my touch would corrupt her, but quickly my selfishness overshadowed that. "I hate that you don't have the freedom of choice."

I had never really wanted a child, I grew up in a home that was so vile and toxic, I knew I wouldn't have the ability to be as impartial as a child deserved to be. Not with the trauma I still hadn't worked through, even after all these years.

And I'd always just been thankful I didn't have to worry about it anymore, but hearing those words from her, understanding her, the reminder that the choice was taken from me burned in my chest. Just because I don't want the experience of parenthood, does not mean that I didn't deserve to make that decision alone.

"Thank you, Darlin'. I'm ok. It's never something I wanted for myself. So I've had time to process." She nodded, absorbing that information carefully. I leaned my head forward, kissing her neck. I wrapped my arms around her waist and gently guided her to move. Her slick heat was not touching my erection, but I felt her warmth and suddenly I was desperate for her to slam down onto me.

Her head fell back as my lips claimed her throat, I forced myself to focus on the soft sound she made as she let her inhibitions go so I couldn't think about biting into her perfect flesh.

Her breasts were arched forward and I couldn't resist taking one of the swollen peaks into my mouth, dancing my tongue around the sensitive area. She gasped and pressed into me further. Her center was flush against me, and she moved back and forth, gliding her slick opening along me and I felt her body tightened with anticipation. My arms tightened around her, urging her to move quicker.

Her breathy moans grew feverishly, then she was lifting up, removing her slickness from me and I nearly protested, but her hand came down to grip me, lining me up so that she could sink down. As she did, our eyes met. Inch by inch she possessed me and the feeling was unrivaled.

How is it that it took me a century to feel comfortable in my body, but only a second to feel so at home in hers?

It was a slow, torturous, delicious descent as she claimed every inch of me with her body. And when she was fully seated, I held her in place. My eyes burned into hers, watching as her lips parted, and her skin flushed.

"You are so beautiful, Athena." I don't know how long we sat there, with me so deep inside of her, unmoving, just gazing into each other's eyes. But I could have continued for a lifetime.

Slowly, she started moving again, and the sensation was divine. It was slow at first, not tentative, but savoring. But as her hips rolled, and her body adjusted to my length, I felt her inner walls tighten around me and I groaned, falling back onto the bed. I looked up at the goddess who was riding me, her red hair falling down her back as her head lulled and she turned her face to the ceiling. I'd never seen something so stunning. If I were a painter, I'd attempt to recreate the look on her face, the way her body fit onto mine so gloriously, but even the most talented artists on this Earth would be unable to capture her. She had the type of beauty that was impossible to recreate. A beauty that many would try and fail to emulate.

"You're staring at me," she mused through a light chuckle and deep moans. Her hips continued their adventurous exploration of me.

"Just trying to memorize this moment," I responded, truthfully. She leaned down until her chest was flush against mine, her warm skin felt like a fire against mine, but I welcomed the burn.

"Then let's make it memorable." Her lips caught mine and she began to move quicker, with reckless abandon. Her smooth movements were replaced by quick, sharp thrusts, and I pushed my hips up to meet hers. Our skin hit against each other as she rode me. My hands drifted from her hips, finding the swollen bud at her apex, her appreciative gasp urged me forward and I moved my fingers in time with her body sliding up and down on me.

I felt her begin to tremble, her release mere inches away. I wanted to give it to her. All of it. My life. My passion. My past. My future. She was the one. The one I'd need for the rest of my life. Nothing had felt right before, and nothing will feel right again, not without her.

The words wouldn't tumble from my lips, so I showed her with my body. Thrusting deeper and harder until she was exploding around me, taking me off the cliff with her. I'd follow her over any edge.

We were a quiet mess of heavy breathing and sweaty bodies, our souls holding onto each other.

I held her closely, the space behind my ribs feeling more alive than it has in decades, and I felt the overwhelming desire to breathe her in, to memorize her scent and her movements. To recall this very moment no matter where life takes me, to know I can think back to this incomparable experience. With her.

She lifted off of me, and I missed the connection instantly. But as she laid down beside me, and snuggled her naked form into my side, nestling her head on my chest, I realized that I craved everything with her. Not just the physical moments that her body belonged to me, and mine to her, but the soft, quiet moments like this. I wanted to wake up next to her, I wanted to make coffee in our kitchen, I wanted to watch tv late into the evening, I wanted long car rides, I wanted grocery runs, I wanted normal. I wanted a life.

I craved the mundane with her.

ATHENA

TWENTY

Yesterday was a dream.

I had the world's most romantic date with Silas, then spent the better part of the night indulging in the quiet ferocity that is Laz. They left just before 3 am, telling me that they needed to leave or they'd monopolize my entire night and I wouldn't get any sleep. I had argued last night, saying that I didn't mind, but sitting here now at work, trying to keep my eyes open. I understand why they had left.

My entire body tingled with the memory of both of their hands, mouths, and bodies claiming me. It was a type of sensual awakening that made me realize how dull my life had been before. Colors were more vibrant, songs were more exciting, and things were different. I was different.

I found myself staring at the pink roses in the vase on the counter. Seeing my newly realized passion in their colors. Smelling my euphoria in their scent. Feeling my freedom in their thorns. I would never look at pink roses the same way again.

The bell above the door rang and I looked up from my daydream to find the lethally handsome and equally dangerous Orpheus walking into my business. Shock was my first reaction. Then confusion. I stood from my stool behind the counter and crossed the floor to him. He wore a dark charcoal suit, his black hair slicked back and his eyes found mine. Burning into me the way they had the day of the tour. I hadn't seen him since that moment. Haven't said a word to him since he heard me reading that book out loud. Since he watched me, writhing between Laz and Silas. Since I looked directly at him and said those words. My face flushed at the memory of his eyes on me from the dark.

"Orpheus, hi," I said timidly, instantly embarrassed by how flustered I sounded. His eyes raked across my body quickly, nearly imperceptible, but I felt the heat of his gaze on my form. My tight jeans and dark emerald green blouse hugged my curves deliciously. I'd dressed this morning with the knowledge and hope that I could very well see one of the wandering newcomers. Thankful that I felt confident and attractive because, under his stare, I was melting.

"Athena," he said quickly, attempting to be devoid of emotion, but I recognized that sort of breathless sound. He was good at hiding it, however, I was just as good at noticing it. That was a strange thought to me, considering I'd only met the guy a few days ago, and spoken to him truly only once.

"How can I help you?" I didn't miss the way his shoulders rose and fell quickly with forced even breaths.

"I'm hoping you can help me find a book." My eyebrows rose. I wondered if Orpheus was a reader. I could see it, but part of me thought that if he read, it wasn't smut and romance that he was spending his time with. He seemed like a non-fiction kind of guy. Some people read to escape the world they live in. I have a sneaking suspicion that Orpheus has trouble letting go of his control, even in his own mind. But I could be wrong.

"That's what I'm here for. Do you know what book you're looking for?" His eyes darkened and he stood incredibly still, I wasn't even sure he was breathing anymore.

"I'm looking for a book about a group of friends who've been together for most of their lives. Have been all each other had for years." I start flipping through the endless catalog of plots in my mind, there were several books like that, with that found family trope. "But then they meet this girl who starts sleeping with several of the friends. She's got them fawning over her." My eyes flick up and lock on his. Understanding washed over me at his words. It was clear what he was doing now. "You see, this girl has the potential to ruin everything this group has worked for. And one of them really doesn't want that to happen. In fact, he'll do whatever he has to ensure that it doesn't." He took a single step forward, but he might as well have been breathing down my neck. His presence was overwhelming.

"How does it end?" I asked, swallowing deeply. Another step.

"That's the thing, I haven't finished it yet." He was close to me now, too close - or not close enough- my mind and body couldn't agree.

"What do you hope will happen?" My tongue darted out to wet my suddenly too-dry lips. His eyes tracked the movement hungrily. His hooded eyes watching me the way he did that day among the stacks.

"That's the problem, there's a part of me that thinks this girl could be good for their group." His eyes scanned my face, darting between my eyes and my mouth.

"But the other part?" I breathed, quietly. I felt the frigid air rolling off of his body and I couldn't help but shiver.

"The other part of me wants the group to have their fill of her and move on, back to their lives." It stung, I couldn't deny that, but I couldn't act on that hurt now. Not when I was so deep under his spell.

"The whole group?" His eyes narrowed at that, heat in his gaze. I bit my lip and a soft growl rumbled in his chest. I felt the vibration of it in my bones. "You want them all to have their fill?" I was too enchanted by this moment to be embarrassed about asking if he wanted me the way the others had.

"I can't decide," he answered quietly. I believed him. His breath was cool on my lips. I took this moment to study his face. It was chiseled and hard. I could see the edge of his jawbone with perfect clarity. His dark eyes had no more color up close than they had from a distance. I was enthralled by him. My body's reaction was eager and needy.

He stood there in silent tension for a few more moments, his eyes watching my mouth with indecision.

"Why were you so afraid?" He asked, his voice still quiet, reserved. He must have seen the confusion on my face because he continued. "At the diner. You were afraid, I'd never felt fear like that before." His tone was almost sympathetic. "Why?"

That broke the spell, slightly. I pushed off of him, my hands meeting the hard planes of his chest with as much force as I could muster.

"That's none of your damn business, Orpheus." He didn't move, it was as if I was pushing against a brick wall. Instead, he gripped one of my wrists and kept my hand against his body. His eyes widened as his skin brushed mine and a shock spread from the point of contact.

"I know that, but you can tell me anyway." I was angry, I was turned on, and I was afraid.

"Let go of me," I screamed, feeling the tell-tale signs of the darkness creeping into my mind. I couldn't breathe.

His hold loosened, but he didn't let me go. The darkness on his face was replaced with worry. "What's wrong?" He sounded concerned but I couldn't focus on that. For a brief moment, the hand on my wrist wasn't Orpheus', it was *his*.

For a moment, I was lost.

It was a cold night, in the middle of winter. I remember the house felt empty because Mom was away at a conference for the weekend. It was the first time I was going to spend some 'quality time' with my stepfather. They'd only started dating a few years ago when I was in middle school and they tied the knot and he moved in just a few months ago. It was a hard adjustment. Adding a new person to our routine. It had just been Mom and me for so long, I resented his presence for a while, but I was happy that she was happy. She'd spent most of her life living for me, I didn't feel right about holding her love hostage. She deserved to feel loved by more than just me. Even if he gave me the creeps.

He was nice enough, but there was just something about the way he looked at me. The way he commented on my clothing like he simultaneously liked what he saw, and hated that I planned on going in public dressed like that.

He'd been harmless.

Until that weekend.

I felt sick after dinner. Like the world was spinning and I couldn't keep up. I went to bed early, trying to combat the dizziness and nausea, but just as I began drifting in and out of consciousness, the door to my room opened. I was stuck somewhere between sleep and reality when I realized he had me pinned beneath his body. His selfish mouth was stealing kisses. Whiskey. I tasted whiskey on his mouth. It was bitter, wrong. I didn't understand it. I couldn't believe it.

I didn't fight back. I couldn't. I was frozen. In fear, in shock, in pain.

He told me that I was his precious little girl. That he loved me. That I had told him I wanted him. With my outfits, and my back talk. He said I was asking to be punished.

He violated me that night in a way no one ever had, and while I wished the drugs had taken the memory of his vile hands and his vicious kisses, nothing could erase the fragmented pictures that would forever be imprinted on my soul.

Panic seized my heart and my breath didn't come. I struggled against Orpheus' hold. Bending at the waist, I pulled my hand from his grip. There was a tightness to my chest like rocks were being piled on top of me and I couldn't escape no matter how hard I fought.

"Athena," a voice sounded, but I couldn't focus on that. The edges of my vision blurred, and images flashed in my mind.

"Athena, please," the voice was strained as if the owner was in as much pain as I was. I felt a pair of cold hands grip my face, but I didn't pull away. Instead, I saw a pair of eyes that didn't haunt me. They were dark black. A comforting sight. "You're safe, I swear it," he cooed, softly, a look of worry on his face. I tried to focus on his words but found the breath was still not coming to my eager lungs.

"Name four things you can see," he demanded. When I didn't respond he held me still, moving his head so that he could hold my eyes. "Four things you can see, Athena. Name them now."

I nodded, drawing in shallow breaths. "Books," I started, feeling the lightheadedness begin. My eyes darted around the space, willing the spinning room to slow so I could focus. "The lamps." I gasped, turning my head aimlessly. Needing to see more. Begging to see more. "The window." My anxious eyes landed on him. "You."

"Three things you can smell." I swallowed deeply, forcing air into my lungs. This time it came. Not easily, but it came.

"My perfume, the pink roses… you." He nodded.

"Good, you're doing well. Now tell me two things you can feel." His hands were soft against the skin of my face. I felt him holding me upright as my mind began to settle. Breath came easier. Everything slowly returned to focus. My eyes adjusted to the space.

"The ground under my feet," I whispered, he nodded urging me on. "You." The room stopped spinning. I felt grounded, firmly planted in reality. The memory locked tightly back in the box I created for him all those years ago.

"And one thing you can taste," Orpheus hadn't let go of my face, his eyes scanned my face furiously. Worry and fear. It had been a very long time since I had a panic attack so vivid, and so painful. Since he had been the star of my memories. Orpheus was a lifeline, holding out a hand for me as I waded through my tumultuous sea of traumatic experiences. My breath evened out, and there was nothing but Orpheus and me.

"You," I whispered before crashing my lips to his. He pushed me off, quickly, still holding my face between his hands. He looked at me with a sort of shocked expression for a moment. I worried that I had crossed a line. Worried that I had taken advantage of his kindness, blurring the lines of his consent. He watched me, a war of emotions crossing his expression. I felt shame and guilt seeping into my chest, but it only lasted for a brief time before a fire lit in his eyes, and throwing caution to the wind he closed the gap between us again, taking my lips with his.

He pulled my face to his, urging me to fully emerge myself in this moment with him. So, I did. My tongue sought out his, tasting him the way I longed to. His hands never left my face, and his body never pressed against mine, but that didn't make the kiss any less passionate. I longed for his comfort.

He tasted like bourbon and ice. A cold shock to my system that only brought me further from the horrors of my past. It was addictive and overwhelming.

He captured my bottom lip between his teeth and bit slightly, not to the point of pain, but it was enough to draw an eager moan from my lips.

I was so oblivious to the world, that I hadn't noticed the door open and the three patrons making their way inside The Maine Plotline, but I felt their gazes burning into my skin.

I forced my eyes to open and saw Laz, Silas, and Samara standing by the front door, their eyes full of seduction and lust.

A brief flash of embarrassment crawled up my spine and I went to push back off of Orpheus. Silas, Laz, and Samara were watching us with hooded expressions, not a trace of anger. Instead, they each looked as if they wanted a taste as well. I blushed deeply.

"Sorry to interrupt," Silas said, cheekily, stepping forward to hand me a single pink rose. Orpheus hadn't turned to face his companions, instead, his gaze was trained on my face as he breathed deeply. I tried to ignore it and grabbed the rose from Silas' outstretched hand.

"Hi, Silas. Thank you." I blushed as his eyes scanned my outfit appreciatively. His tongue traced his bottom lip, across that delicious piercing there.

"I told you that I wanted a few minutes with her," Orpheus addressed his friends without turning to them.

"We couldn't wait," Laz admitted sheepishly.

"I wasn't expecting you all," I said, the double meaning was obviously clear.

I didn't expect them to be here tonight, but it was more than that. I didn't expect them in my life, in my bed, in my mind. My soul. These four people had laid a claim to a piece of me and I didn't know why, or how, but they did. And I never wanted them to let go.

"I told them about what you spoke to me about yesterday," Silas started. "About the asshole's friend from the bar." I sighed, still feeling so raw from the panic attack that even the thought of Louis was threatening to send me back over the edge. The slightest hitch in my breath drew their attention.

Orpheus' fingers found my chin, drawing my gaze to his face.

"Stay with me," he commanded. It was a soft request, but it was what I needed. I nodded, feeling the call of the void slip away.

"Thanks," I whispered to him as he dropped his fingers from my face. I looked over at the others who were waiting with patient expressions on their faces.

"Greg, um, Louis's friend, came to see me. He says Louis is missing. My friend Davia told me that he even went to the police. It was too early to report him missing then, but if he still isn't home, then it's only a matter of time before he goes back and police start asking around." I swallowed deeply, hating the idea of being at the center of yet another investigation. The cops in this town didn't prove to be sympathetic to a victim back then, so I can't imagine they would now.

"So, you're worried about being questioned?" Samara asked, taking a few steps forward. I shook my head.

"I didn't tell Davia the truth about what happened that night." I held the long stem of the rose in my hand and twirled it mindlessly as I continued. "I didn't want her to feel guilty for leaving me alone with him."

A few deep rumbling growls sounded in the room. It was a possessive sound, an angry sound. "Shouldn't she?" Orpheus said, his eyes were dark and unrelenting.

"No, she shouldn't," I said, an edge of annoyance in my tone.

"She left you with a rapist," he added as if I didn't know what had happened to me. As if I hadn't been replaying it every night since. "Sounds like a shitty friend." I was seeing red. Seething. "He got his chance because she left you alone and vulnerable." Orpheus was pissed, his fists clenching at his sides. I felt something snap, pain, and anger that had been building for a decade rushed to the surface.

"She was one of the only people who believed me when it happened the first time!" I yelled, tears pricking my eyes. That shut him up. Shut them all up. Their eyes were locked on me, the silence so potent I felt like it could detonate at any moment. "When the whole town turned on me, choosing to take *his* word over mine, turning me into a social pariah, she stood by me. She kept me grounded, kept me sane. When the cops and the town turned it all back on me when they tried to tell me that it was my fault when they tried to tell me that I was lying, seeking attention, she stood by me. She told me they were wrong!" I was a blubbering mess, falling apart before their eyes, but I didn't care. "When their voices were so loud, she was right there drowning them out. She was there for me, feeling every ounce of my pain right alongside me. So no, she doesn't deserve to feel guilt over this when it's not her fucking fault that that asshole was a rapist. And I don't want to hear you blame a woman for a man's actions ever again." Orpheus' eyes softened as he listened. "Do you understand me?" It was so silent, you could have heard a tear hit the ground. Nobody moved for a moment and I let the tears fall down my face, unrestrained. I'd spent too long hiding my emotions, and I was tired of it.

Samara was the first to move, her arms encircled me and pulled me into her body for an embrace. I dissolved into the hold, letting her stroke my hair. My hands balled into her clothes as I nestled my face into the crook of her neck.

After a minute or two, I was composed again, my tears had dried up and I felt a little lighter than I had before. I pulled back, looking up into Samara's brown eyes, expecting to see pity. But it wasn't pity I saw in her expression, it was a softer emotion, a deeper one. Her cold hand came up to cup my cheek and she leaned forward planting the softest kiss on my lips. It was brief, barely a kiss, but it meant everything to me at that moment. When she pulled back she smiled sadly at me, an unreadable expression on her face.

Samara stepped away, and I looked over at Orpheus for the first time since my outburst, he wore an expression of shame, and I hated it.

"I'm sorry," I whispered, and Orpheus was standing in front of me in an instant. Faster than he should have been able to.

"Don't apologize to me or anyone else for making your boundaries known, Athena. Ever." His dark eyes bore into mine and I nodded.

"I'm sorry for what happened to you, Darlin'," Laz offered from their spot near the door. I smiled sweetly at them and turned to see Silas who was seething.

"Who the fuck was it?" He asked through gritted teeth, his eyes an almost unnatural shade of red.

"He's in prison. It's ok." That seemed to placate him, a little.

"He was convicted?" Samara asked, gently. I shook my head.

"Not for what he did to me," I admitted, sheepishly. "Turns out, he was embezzling money from The Maine Plotline." I shook my head, that was such a horrific time of our lives. We nearly had to close the doors. We had no idea where the money was going, no idea why we couldn't seem to keep our heads above water. I remember the day they took him away in the police car. It felt like a hollow victory. On one hand, he was going away, being punished for his crimes. On the other, it didn't escape me that if he hadn't committed that entirely different crime, he would never have been held accountable for what he did to me. "I'm ok, I promise," I said, hoping it was convincing.

"So, what would you like us to say, should the authorities come to speak to us?" Laz asked, changing the subject. I mouthed 'thank you' to them and they nodded.

"I told Davia that you all saw Louis and I leave the bar and once outside we went our separate ways." Laz nodded, but the others looked furious. "Listen, I know I should have told the truth, but honestly, I can't be a victim again. I barely survived it last time in this town. The rumors, the judging." I felt my hand tighten around the stem of the rose. "I can't do that again, ok?" A sharp pain stung my palm. I winced, pulling my hand away from the rose, seeing the spot where a thorn had dug into my palm. I turned to the counter, feeling the blood pooling, and began to spill down my arm, dripping onto the pink petals of the rose, marring it with the red hue of my blood. I placed the rose on the counter, and reached for a tissue, using it to apply pressure to the wound. The pain was there, but dull. It was deep, but not deep enough that I would need stitches.

When I returned my gaze to my visitors, my heart skipped a beat and fear seized my heart.

I didn't see the handsome and beautiful strangers from the bar, or the soft and comforting faces of the people I've kissed, and made love to.

What was staring back at me were four ravenous creatures. Their eyes were blood red, dark veins running along their faces. Their ears were pointed, sticking out from their messy hair. Long, vicious fangs protruded from their gums, glistening violently in the warm glow of the lamps. Long claws stood ready for attack at their sides.

A scream caught in my throat, my heart pumping quicker than it had any right to.

"What.. what are you?" I gasped, my fight or flight instinct utterly broke, settling on the third option…freeze.

The four of them stalked forward, moving toward me in some kind of slow methodical hunt. I was their prey.

A raspy, violent sound ripped from their throats. A single word, spoken in terrifying unison, had my entire body clenching in fear and uncertainty.

"Mate."